Dear Reader,

What could be more romantic than a wedding? Picture the bride in an exquisite gown, with flowers cascading from the glorious bouquet in her hand. Imagine the handsome groom in a finely tailored tuxedo, his eyes sparkling with happiness and love. Hear them promise "to have and to hold" each other forever. . . . This is the perfect ending to a courtship, the blessed ritual we cherish in our hearts. And now, in honor of the tradition of June brides, we present a month's line-up of six LOVESWEPTs with beautiful brides and gorgeous grooms on the covers.

Don't miss any of our brides and grooms this month:

#552 HER VERY OWN BUTLER
     by Helen Mittermeyer
#553 ALL THE WAY by Gail Douglas
#554 WHERE THERE'S A WILL . . .
     by Victoria Leigh
#555 DESERT ROSE by Laura Taylor
#556 RASCAL by Charlotte Hughes
#557 ONLY YOU by Bonnie Pega

There's no better way to celebrate the joy of weddings than with all six LOVESWEPTs, each one a fabulous love story written by only the best in the genre!

With best wishes,

Nita Taublib
Associate Publisher/LOVESWEPT

WHAT ARE *LOVESWEPT* ROMANCES?

They are stories of true romance and touching emotion. We believe those two very important ingredients are constants in our highly sensual and very believable stories in the *LOVESWEPT* line. Our goal is to give you, the reader, stories of consistently high quality that may sometimes make you laugh, sometimes make you cry, but are always fresh and creative and contain many delightful surprises within their pages.

Most romance fans read an enormous number of books. Those they truly love, they keep. Others may be traded with friends and soon forgotten. We hope that each *LOVESWEPT* romance will be a treasure—a "keeper." We will always try to publish

LOVE STORIES YOU'LL NEVER FORGET
BY AUTHORS YOU'LL ALWAYS REMEMBER

The Editors

Laura Taylor
Desert Rose

BANTAM BOOKS

NEW YORK · TORONTO · LONDON · SYDNEY · AUCKLAND

DESERT ROSE

A Bantam Book / July 1992

ISBN 0-553-44234-1

Published simultaneously in the United States and Canada

Bantam Books are published by Bantam Books, a division of
Bantam Doubleday Dell Publishing Group, Inc. Its trademark,
consisting of the words "Bantam Books" and the portrayal of
a rooster, is Registered in U.S. Patent and Trademark Office
and in other countries. Marca Registrada. Bantam Books, 666
Fifth Avenue, New York, New York 10103.

PRINTED IN THE UNITED STATES OF AMERICA

OPM   0 9 8 7 6 5 4 3 2 1

This one's for Patty and Duane, two very important people in our cherished Marine Corps family.

Author Note: The FA-18 (a fighter attack jet also known as the F-18) is normally a single-seat aircraft, but the FA-18D model utilized by the United States Marine Corps has been structurally altered to accommodate a two-man crew for a variety of purposes, including visual reconnaissance missions.

Prologue

David Winslow dreamed with all of his senses engaged. He craved the warmth and willingness of a silken-skinned woman, an eighteen-ounce rare steak, and a six-pack of ice-cold beer. Preferably American beer. All the things he couldn't have during the endless days of isolation and long nights haunted by fear, hunger, and loneliness.

Sprawled across an evil-smelling pallet that didn't accommodate his large-framed body, he shifted restlessly in his sleep. He groaned, the ache in his empty stomach nearly as severe as the ache in his loins.

Reaching out, David sought comfort where none existed. He found nothing more substantial than air. Disappointment and frustration made him groan a second time.

A volley of rifle shots suddenly exploded in the courtyard adjacent to his cellblock.

Instantly alert, he jerked upward to a seated

position. He automatically crossed his arms in front of his face and upper torso, ready to defend himself from any threat. His chest heaved, the air raging in and out of his body scalding his lungs as he scanned the shadowed corners of his small cell through narrowed eyes.

David scowled and brought himself under control. He kept his body still and shallowed his breathing as he listened for the subtlest hint that he might no longer be the sole occupant of the cellblock.

Several tense minutes passed.

Finally convinced that he was alone, he forced himself to his feet and prowled his cell like the caged animal he felt he'd become. He remained in motion for nearly an hour, the exercise tiring but also an integral part of his morning ritual.

David eventually paused in front of his make-shift calendar. He simmered with renewed fury as he stared at the grooves he'd already made in the wall with a metal tab removed from a zipper on his flight suit. Digging into his pocket, he fingered the sharpened tab and resigned himself to making the fifty-seventh mark.

Fighting the despair that throbbed inside him as he completed his task, David returned to his pallet. As he sat, his spine rigid and his fists clenched so tightly that they ached, he fought for a mental state somewhere between self-pity and hopefulness.

He longed for the luxury of companionship and conversation, just as he longed for decent food, a hot shower, and clean clothes. He whispered a prayer for freedom, but he wondered if anyone would ever respond to his fervent entreaty.

David closed his eyes, bowed his head, and massaged the back of his neck. He calmed himself yet again with deep breaths and vowed to survive in spite of the odds stacked against him.

An observer, he suspected, would have understood and empathized with his frustration, his loneliness, and his fear of being executed without a trial, but he knew that his captors would never permit an observer, not even one from the Red Cross.

Instead, David Winslow, a defiantly stubborn thirty-five-year-old aviator, American citizen, and officer in the United States Marine Corps who refused to succumb to starvation or to surrender to the other acts of violence inflicted upon him by his guards, consciously and steadfastly endured.

An unexpected sound jarred David from his thoughts. He quickly stood and moved into the shadowed corner of his cell. Tension tightened every muscle of his body when he heard more than one set of footsteps racing down the cell-block's center aisle.

Squaring his shoulders, David worked at mastering his anxiety over the prospect of yet another session with his interrogators. He counted each second that passed. A fine sheen of perspiration covering his face, he grimaced and recalled the beatings he'd experienced during the first weeks of his captivity.

Raking a hand through his dark hair, David froze when the barred door next to his cell was pushed open. One of the guards shouted in Arabic, his ire evident. David took a shallow breath, then another.

He heard someone, and then some thing, land on the cell floor. The barred door closed, the squealing resistance of the rusty tracks a lingering punctuation mark in the otherwise silent cellblock. The guards quickly departed without even glancing in his direction.

Bewildered, he gave in to his curiosity and cautiously moved out of the corner. He slid along the wall, but the sound of sobbing brought him up short. He exhaled, compassion and comprehension taking the edge off his surprise.

Understanding the man's need for privacy, he remained silent as he stood there. He would give his fellow prisoner time to compose himself, time to come to terms with the shock and horror he felt. David leaned back against the wall, closed his eyes, and wondered if they spoke a common language.

"This can't be happening."

He stiffened, unable to believe his ears.

"This *cannot* be happening to me," the female voice groaned again through her weeping.

A woman? An English-speaking woman? He shook his head. He was losing it, he realized. He'd dreamed about the soft embrace of a woman on a nightly basis, and he'd finally been reduced to fantasizing that one occupied the adjacent cell.

He tried to speak, tried to verify her existence, but each time he opened his mouth, words failed him. Disgusted with his own uncertainty and afraid that he'd manufactured a companion out of desperation, he retreated to his pallet.

David moved soundlessly, his entire body shaking as he marshaled his thoughts and pondered his options. Her sobbing eventually abated, and he welcomed the respite from her shattered emotions. His own emotions, he realized, were unsettled enough.

Still, disbelief and doubt lingered within him, and he felt compelled to make certain that he hadn't imagined her.

"Are you all right?" David Winslow finally asked, his voice low and rough from lack of use.

One

"Are you all right?"

The question came out of nowhere, startling Emma so thoroughly that she dropped the tote bag she clutched against her chest. Certain that she'd imagined the masculine voice, she groaned, "Oh, God."

"Can you hear me?" he asked again. "Are you all right?"

Wondering if she'd crossed the fine line that separated sanity and insanity, she tilted her head to one side and listened as she knelt on the filthy floor of her cell.

"We'll do this one more time."

Emma found the mellow resonance of his deep voice reassuring, but she still didn't quite trust her own ears.

"Are you all right?"

"Who's there?" she whispered, finally believing that she wasn't alone.

"David Winslow. Major, United States Marine Corps."

"You're kidding!"

"Don't I wish," he responded before he chuckled wryly.

"What . . . how . . . I don't understand."

"Take a deep breath and settle down, miss," he advised, his humor vanishing. "When you can think clearly, I want you to tell me your name."

"Emma," she said after taking the steadying breath he'd suggested. "Emma Hamilton."

"Are you all right, Emma Hamilton? Have you been injured in any way?"

She didn't even attempt to varnish the truth. "My pride's dented, I'm scared out of my mind, and I'd kill for a shower, clean clothes, and a way out of this nightmare I'm having." Emma swallowed the panic she felt rising inside her. "It isn't a nightmare, is it? I'm really in a jail."

"I'm afraid so." David paused, then asked, "Where are you from?"

"San Diego," she replied, relieved to be asked a question she could actually answer, and even more relieved that this man sounded so . . . normal.

"A California girl, huh?"

"Sorry to disappoint you, but I left my bikini at home, and my hair's jet black."

"Shucks."

She laughed at his teasing and briefly forgot her fear that she wouldn't ever see her family again. "What about you? Where are you from?"

"Billings, Montana. Born, bred, and educated there."

Amazed, she said, "A cowboy?"

"A Marine, miss."

She heard his pride and found it endearing, but a wisp of suspicion unexpectedly filtered into her consciousness. "This isn't some kind of a trick, is it? Did the secret police put you in here to test me?"

She waited for him to answer, but his silence made her start to wonder if he would ever speak to her again. She urged, "Please don't stop talking to me. I'm . . . I'm holding on to my wits with my fingernails right now, and I really need to believe you're real."

"I've been thinking that the secret police put *you* in here," David admitted.

Emma nodded and tried to sound in control of her emotions. "I guess that's understandable." Curious, she asked, "So, what are you really doing here?"

"Counting the days," he quipped, but the anger edging his voice made his attempt at levity fall flat.

"Americans aren't exactly welcome in this particular part of the world," she said. "Unless, of course, we happen to be providing food and medical supplies."

"That much I've already figured out."

"Do you work for the CIA?"

He laughed suddenly, the sound rich and warm and surprisingly seductive. "Now I know you aren't a plant. You're too blunt."

Emma didn't appreciate his observation, having been accused for years, especially by her diplomat brother, Sam, of having little or no tact. Nor was she prepared for the underlying sensuality in his laughter, which made her fumble for her next comment. "I guess you aren't allowed to discuss your . . . mission, are you?"

The humor remained in his voice. "Reconnaissance isn't considered a secret when routine visual recon missions are agreed upon by both sides."

"Then you're a pilot?"

"Second seat of an FA-18D."

"Second seat?"

"Behind the pilot. I'm a Weapons Systems Officer," David clarified.

"I don't know a lot about military airplanes."

He chuckled. "Most people don't, but I won't take it personally."

A door suddenly squeaked open and slammed against a wall at the far end of the corridor, followed by footsteps advancing toward her cell. Emma was jerked back to the reality of imprisonment. She stiffened, and an apprehensive moan escaped her. "David?" she whispered.

"Stay calm and be very quiet, Emma. It's the safest thing to do with these people."

Shaken by the possibility of additional interrogation, she admitted, "I don't think I'll ever feel safe again, and I'm starting to wonder if I'll ever feel anything but fear."

She heard David mutter a harsh curse, but he didn't say anything more to her. She remained on the floor in the center of her cell. As she knelt there, her mind filled with images of cruelty and violence, Emma suddenly wondered how long David Winslow had been incarcerated.

The guard paused in front of Emma's cell. Her heart thundered against her ribs as she kept her eyes fastened on the scuffed surface of the boots he wore. Hugging her tote bag, she breathed a silent prayer and remained very still.

The guard finally moved on, paused in front of what Emma assumed was David's cell, lingered there for several silent minutes, and then retraced his footsteps. She breathed normally only after she heard the cellblock door slam shut.

"Emma?"

"Yes?" She loathed the quiver in her voice, but she couldn't stem the tide of anxiety that threatened to engulf her. The consequences of imprisonment in a Middle East country considered a renegade by the rest of the world were almost too shocking to grasp fully.

"The guards check the cells nearly every hour. You've just experienced routine rounds. That guy's one of the regulars in this cellblock."

Emma forced herself to speak. "I'll have to trust you."

He hesitated, then cautioned, "We'll have to trust each other as long as we're in here together."

She started to shake. She couldn't stop the violent trembling of her body or the sudden chattering of her teeth.

"Talk to me, Emma," David ordered sharply.

"It'll help you deal with the stress. If you're having the shakes, try getting up and moving around your cell. You can walk off the tension you're feeling. It's normal, so don't start thinking that you're cracking up, because you're not. I experienced the same thing you're going through right now when I first checked into this hotel from hell."

She took a deep breath, grateful for the compassion she heard in his rough voice, but she lacked the strength to move just yet. "I think I'd rather listen for now, if that's okay with you. I'm still a little too shaky to do much chatting or hiking."

"You need to know the rules around here. I've discovered that these guys aren't real patient if you don't observe them. Understand?"

"Tell me the rules, David."

"Don't ever initiate conversation of any kind, not unless you're prepared to confess to whatever crimes they're accusing you of having committed. Always keep your eyes averted unless ordered to do otherwise. Study a shoulder or a spot on the wall when they speak to you or if you have to answer a question. These guys consider prisoners and women second-class citizens."

"How enlightened of them," she croaked.

"Have you been interrogated?" he asked in a somber tone that hinted at his familiarity with the experience.

She nodded absently, forgetting for a moment that they weren't face-to-face.

"Emma?"

"Sorry. Yes, I've been interrogated. They started

around dusk yesterday and kept hammering at me all night long and then most of this morning. . . ." Her voice splintered as she recalled the terror of being bound to a chair and questioned endlessly by a series of uniformed men who appeared to possess about as much humanity as a pile of rocks. She suppressed a shudder. "I still don't understand why they think I'm some kind of a spy. I haven't done anything wrong."

"You're tired, aren't you?"

"Yes," she choked out, tears welling in her eyes at the tender concern in his voice.

"And you're more frightened than you ever thought you could be."

"Totally."

"Me too."

"You don't sound scared," she accused, suddenly jealous of and resentful at his composure. "In fact you sound very calm and collected."

"I've just had more practice at this. Fear and fatigue work in their favor, Emma," he quietly reminded her. "The secret is to use their system against them. Never challenge your captors overtly, simply undermine their tactics."

She slowly responded to his patience, rational advice, and the measured quality of his deep voice. She would try, she promised herself, to imitate his calmness, even though she felt anything but calm. "How do you know all this stuff?"

"Survival school. It's mandatory for all aviators."

He paused. She sensed that he was weighing his

words carefully. She wondered why, but she didn't press him. She also wondered about David Winslow, the man. Because she couldn't see him, she found herself speculating on his appearance. His voice implied that he was a large man. Not a pretty man, she decided, but rugged and big and broad-shouldered. Emma sighed. She felt safer somehow with his sturdy image forming in her mind.

"Look, I'll teach you as much as I can, but I doubt you'll need the lessons. Keeping a woman in this hellhole isn't real bright, but then I'm not too impressed with their concept of military behavior. Half the people I've encountered here are inept or inexperienced. The rest are just plain mean." David exhaled, the sound weighted with the experience of captivity. "They'll probably just feed you poorly for a few days, try to intimidate you, and then release you to one of the embassies on good terms with the U.S."

"What about you?"

"Don't worry about me," he stated flatly. "There's no percentage in it."

"But I know you exist. If they put us next to each other, perhaps they have other plans for us. Maybe they intend to use us as the star attractions in some horrendous media event."

"Don't anticipate the worst. Just plan for it."

"Is that an old Montana saying?"

"Just common sense."

She smiled. "I've been told I lack that particular characteristic."

"Really."

"Yes. Sam thinks I'm hopeless, but then I suspect he believes that all women are hopeless."

"Sam?"

"The bane of my existence."

"Sounds like a strange relationship," he observed coolly.

"Your typical love-hate, but I secretly adore him."

"I don't like the guy already."

Emma laughed softly, affectionately. "He's all right, just opinionated."

"You deserve better."

Startled by his sharpness, she pointed out, "You don't know me well enough to know what I deserve. Sam's like any—"

"You're right," he broke in, his voice filled with cold resentment. "I don't know you at all."

"—big brother," she whispered to herself as she shrank from David's sudden brusqueness. She felt tense and uncertain again. What had she said to provoke such an abrupt change in him?

"Try to rest, but don't use sleep as an escape from what's happening in here. Whenever you're awake, move around your cell. Exercise is crucial for a positive state of mind. Keep your circulation flowing and your body strong, even if you don't get much to eat. It'll help distract you when the hours drag."

"I'm hungry," she admitted in a small voice as she absently smoothed her long black hair away from her face.

"Don't feel alone, Emma, but don't expect too

much either. The menu is limited to boiled vege-
tables in a watered-down broth, crusts of bread,
that kind of thing. I've had rice a few times, but
not with any regularity, so don't count on it.
Service is erratic, but somebody usually shows up
with what passes for food around here at least
once a day. I've lost some weight. You might too."

Emma pondered his comments as she worked
her hair into a loose braid that trailed down the
center of her back. Although amazed by David's
generosity, she welcomed the information he willingly provided in a steady, matter-of-fact voice.

She liked him, she realized, and she appreciated
his willingness to share his strength, though he
probably needed all of it himself to survive.

"How long have you been here?" she finally
asked.

"Too damn long!"

"How long, David?"

"Fifty-seven days."

Stunned by his reply and amazed by his endurance, she released a ragged sigh. Nearly two months
of captivity, and David Winslow still possessed
courage and the ability to be compassionate to a
total stranger.

Emma finally found her voice. "Have you been
allowed to speak to anyone from a friendly embassy?"

He didn't respond.

"David?"

"No," he ground out. "They haven't let me speak
to anyone. You're the first"—he made a strange

sound—"the first person I've spoken to since I was brought here."

"Thank you."

"For what?"

She smiled. "For being so patient with me. You could've ignored me, and I wouldn't have blamed you."

"That's not my style, Emma."

The gruffness in his voice made her want to hug him. She promised herself that she would someday. "I've already sensed that about you," she said softly.

She heard him clear his throat, then the sound of his footsteps as he paced back and forth in his cell. Uncertain what to say next, she shifted and tried to find a comfortable position while she waited for him to speak to her again.

Because her jeans and blouse were already soiled, Emma didn't dwell on the grimy condition of the cell's floor. Instead she tugged her cape around her shoulders like a shawl to ward off the damp winter chill and reminded herself to take deep breaths each time she felt a wave of fear.

"Emma?"

"Yes?"

"They didn't . . . you weren't . . . help me out here, will you?"

She suddenly understood his uncertain query. "I wasn't raped, David, although . . . for a whiie I thought I might be. They just terrorized me by hauling me around like a sack of grain when I wasn't tied up in a wooden chair in the interrogation room."

"That's something to be thankful for," he reminded her.

"What about you? Did they hurt you?"

"It doesn't matter."

"Of course it matters!" she exclaimed. "Tell me the truth, David. Were you mistreated? I know that kind of thing happens. I heard men being tortured. So don't think lying to me will make me feel any better, because it won't."

"They knocked me around at first, but I've pretty much healed."

His negligent tone aroused her concern. "What did they do to you?"

"They took turns punching me, slapping me, and kicking me," he admitted reluctantly. "The usual in this type of a situation."

"The usual," she echoed in disbelief. "Perhaps it's 'the usual' with some back-alley criminal element, but not among civilized people capable of talking to one another. I don't care how different cultures are," she insisted heatedly, "violence isn't necessary and shouldn't ever be condoned. Were you given medical care?"

"Emma, relax." His voice reflected his amazement at her outburst. "You can't change what's already happened. Besides, a medic dropped by, reset my dislocated shoulder, and cleaned me up. My nose was broken," he added almost as an afterthought, "and it wouldn't stop bleeding."

"How is it now?" she questioned in her determined tone. It was one she used with intransigent government officials she'd dealt with around the world in her work with refugees.

"Crooked, I suspect," he joked.

She sensed that he'd suffered far more than he was willing to admit. "It'll give your face added character," she assured him with a bravado that amazed her. She sensed that she had just entered into an intimate relationship with David Winslow, despite the fact that they couldn't see or touch each another.

"Or scare all the kids in my neighborhood."

She laughed at the wry note in his voice. "I like your attitude, David Winslow."

"Self-pity won't cut it in here. I figured that out right away."

"Remind me of that if I start acting like a baby."

She shivered, suddenly aware that the old adage Only the strong survive would undoubtedly be tested in the hours and days ahead. Emma offered a silent prayer that she would find strength within herself to endure the uncertainty she faced.

"You may be somewhat untested, Emma, but you don't strike me as the baby type."

"I hope not," she replied as she rubbed her arms and shivered beneath her shawl. "I sincerely hope not, David. I wouldn't want to disappoint you."

Two

Unable to sleep despite the late hour, David listened to the sporadic bursts of gunfire from automatic weapons and the periodic grenade explosions that punctuated the night. He no longer felt alarmed by the familiar sounds of violence, just a weary kind of resignation that seemed to permeate his soul.

David suspected that the skirmishes between troops loyal to the government and the various political factions that controlled segments of the capital city would continue until the country's dictator was overthrown and replaced by elected officials. Until then he expected to remain a prisoner, a potential bargaining chip to be used, or perhaps eventually discarded, depending upon the political climate of the Middle East.

He exhaled heavily and closed his large hands into fists, frustration gnawing on his nerves as he racked his brain yet again for a means of escape.

Barring a minor miracle, he already knew that no successful route existed. Diplomacy would be his sole savior.

Restless and on edge, David abandoned his pallet and paced. He allowed himself the luxury of thinking about his family for a few moments, although he understood how self-destructive it was to linger on the emotional stress his status as missing-in-action must inflict on his mother and sister. Deeply concerned about them, he knew they wouldn't give up hope and wouldn't stop praying for his safe return.

He shifted his thoughts to Emma Hamilton and felt once more the unexpected hunger she aroused in him. He didn't know the reasons for her imprisonment. He simply assumed that she'd been in the wrong place at the wrong time. He intended to learn the facts, but he wanted to give her time to adjust to the situation before he broached the subject with her.

Emma.

Not a common or contemporary name, he mused, but he already knew that she possessed uncommon qualities. He'd heard the compassion and gentleness in her voice, as well as her understandable fear. He also sensed her warmth, and he silently craved a large dose of it for himself.

An air-raid siren screamed in the distance as David paused at the thick wall that separated their cells. He pressed both hands flat against the rough-textured surface, as though to absorb the essence of her for a few moments. Pressing his forehead to the wall, he closed his eyes and whispered, "Emma." He savored the very sound of her name.

He half smiled as he recalled her genuine outrage that he'd been harmed by their captors. She brought to mind the image of a fiercely tender kitten. She also renewed his hunger for laughter and physical intimacy, although he grasped the futility of the latter, more elemental impulse.

Still, he wanted to hold her, to soothe her with more than words. He also longed to be soothed and satisfied by her, to lose himself, however briefly, in her warmth and in her body. Desire made him hard, and he breathed a low, lethal-sounding word as he struggled with his frustration.

Because their alliance was founded on uncertainty and a fear of the unknown, and because of a man named Sam, he knew he couldn't expect anything more than friendly conversation from Emma Hamilton, even if the dense wall of mortar and stone blocks separating them somehow magically disappeared.

He groaned quietly and threw back his head. Unable to dismiss the desire flowing relentlessly through him and infusing his imagination, he wondered how he could feel so hotly aroused by the voice of a woman he'd never even seen. But what little he knew about Emma prompted him to imagine her as a shapely, slim-limbed woman of medium height with yards and yards of long, coal-black hair.

Her voice hinted at her age. Twenty-five, no more than thirty. Her skin must be sun-kissed and as soft as satin, and he tortured himself with thoughts of what it would be like to trace every curve and hollow of her body, to linger at pink-tipped breasts that would fill his hands and seduce his lips before his fingertips traveled lower to measure the width of her rounded hips.

Trembling, he jerked away from the barrier that separated him from Emma and began to pace his cell again. He couldn't allow himself to indulge in such fantasies. He tried to force himself to ignore his awareness of her but didn't succeed.

Lost in thought, David flinched when he heard a feminine cry of distress. He paused in mid-stride, tension stiffening his spine and tautening the muscles in his body.

Emma screamed again, the sound chilling David's blood. Had she lied to him? he suddenly wondered. Had the guards or her interrogators done more than shove her around and question her for endless hours?

"Help me," she moaned in her sleep.

"Emma! Wake up. You're having a nightmare."

"Help me," she pleaded.

David gripped the iron bars of his cell and called out, "Emma, listen to me. I can't get to you. You have to wake up on your own. Fight the nightmare, and wake yourself up. Do it now!" he ordered.

She continued to groan and mumble, but David couldn't make out any of the words. "Emma!

Come on, babe, fight the nightmare," he coaxed, his voice steady despite his worry that she would draw the attention of the guards. "Fight back, Emma. Do it for me, please. Don't give in to your fear." He paused briefly to gauge the impact of his words.

"I'm all right," she gasped.

"Talk to me, babe. It'll help."

"I can't."

He heard her sobbing and understood how alone she felt. Still gripping the iron bars, he said, "I'd hold you if I could."

"I . . . I warned you I'd be a big baby."

"You're not a baby."

"You're just trying to make me feel better."

"I wouldn't lie to you, Emma."

"I woke you, didn't I?"

"I wasn't asleep. I think I've turned into an insomniac since I've been in here."

"Is it always so dark?" she asked plaintively.

David recalled how much the constant darkness had bothered him at first. He felt great empathy for Emma. She still had so much to learn about captivity.

"I'm afraid so, babe."

She sighed, the sound sad enough to make a grown man weep. David very nearly did, then swore at the circumstances that thwarted his desire to hold and comfort her.

"I was having a nightmare."

"I suspected as much."

"I'm really sorry."

"No sweat, Emma. It happens. I didn't sleep too well my first few nights in here either."

"You're so blasted patient and understanding!" she charged, her emotions seesawing back and forth.

"Is there another choice?" he asked in a voice as hard as granite. He couldn't let her tumble into a vat of self-pity. He knew the risk of drowning in it.

"Sam would approve of you."

"I take it that wasn't a compliment," David teased, although the mere mention of the man in her life set his teeth on edge.

"As superior as Sam can be, I miss him."

He sidestepped the dismay her remark inspired. "Focus on getting out of here and going home to him."

Bewildered, she asked, "Why would I go home to Sam? He lives in Paris, and I live in San Diego. Besides, it'll be a cold day in hell before I admit to my brother that I got myself arrested in a foreign country. I'd never hear the end of it."

Sam was her brother? David experienced a wave of relief that Sam wasn't her lover.

"Take a deep breath, why don't you? You've had a nightmare, but you're all right now. You're probably feeling a little disoriented at the moment, but that's perfectly natural."

"David?"

He heard her uncertainty, and he ached to gather her into his arms. "I'm here," he assured her. "Did you save some of the water the guard brought with your meal?"

He waited for her to respond. A minute of silence passed, and David felt his patience flee in the face of his concern for her well-being.

"Answer me, Emma. Your head doesn't rattle when you shake it, so I don't know when, or if, you're nodding."

"Yes!" she snapped, obviously stung by his criticism. "I saved some of the water. That's what you told me to do, so I did it."

"That's a good girl," David said soothingly, ignoring her response. "Have a sip and then move around your cell. Exercise is the key to your survival. I wasn't kidding about that when we talked earlier. Your brain will get mushy if you let your body get weak."

"I'm not some brainless twit who doesn't have the sense to come in out of the rain. Furthermore, I'm not a girl," she announced, her footsteps punctuating each word as she briskly paced back and forth in her cell. "I'm twenty-six years of age. I own my own home, I vote, I can have a glass of wine if I want, and I'm old enough to use good judgment where men and sex are concerned. Any questions, *Major* Winslow?"

He smiled, absurdly proud of her outburst. He knew now that she wasn't caving in over a bad dream. "No questions at the moment, babe, but don't stop moving around that cell. I want to hear your footsteps."

"You're starting to remind me of a nun I used to know," she complained as she kept pacing.

"Talk while you walk, Emma. Tell me what you're feeling right now."

She ignored him. "We called her Sister Mary Drill Instructor. She was *not* my favorite person."

He chuckled. "How are you feeling?"

"Furious. Absolutely furious."

"Of course you are," he agreed. "That's normal. Use your anger, Emma. Make it work for you, babe. I know you can do it."

She made a noise that sounded like an unladylike snort. "If you don't stop calling me *babe*, I may deck you just for the heck of it."

He laughed again. "Be my guest, babe."

"Don't you dare make fun of me."

He smothered the laughter that rumbled through his chest and shook his broad shoulders. "Stay mad, Emma. I don't mind being your target."

His humor slowly waned, and he didn't prod her when she fell silent. Instead, he leaned against the bars of his cell and pondered Emma's feisty nature. Desire throbbed steadily in his loins, and he allowed himself to speculate on the passion she would bring to a lover.

"David?" she said softly a few minutes later.

Roughly shoving his hands through hair that had grown longer than was acceptable to any self-respecting, spit-and-polish Marine Corps officer, he roused himself from his insane fantasies. "You can't believe that this has happened to you, can you?"

Startled, she asked, "How do you always know what I'm thinking?"

"I'll *never* forget my first few days in here," David responded bitterly. "Never."

He recalled the pain of repeated beatings, as well as his haunting fear that he wouldn't survive the abuse or the isolation of imprisonment. Exhaling quietly, he cleared away the vivid memories by sheer force of will.

"Emma, what in hell are you doing in this war-ravaged country?"

"I'm a caseworker for Child Feed. We supply food, clothing, and medical care to children displaced by war. Following the cease-fire a team of our doctors and nurses arrived to set up refugee camps. Since we're a multinational aid group, we frequently work under the auspices of the United Nations."

Pleased that he'd found a way to distract her, David responded to his own curiosity about her work. "How did you happen to become involved with the organization?"

"My dad's a pediatrician. He helped found Child Feed almost twenty years ago after a trip to India. My mother does an annual fund-raiser for Child Feed. She owns an art gallery in San Diego, so she comes into contact with a lot of wealthy types with fairly strong humanitarian instincts. Sam used to work with us, but he's with the State Department now. My younger sister's a nurse, and she periodically donates her time too."

"Sounds like you're all very dedicated," he mused thoughtfully.

"We are, but only because we want to be. Dad never put any pressure on us. I didn't get involved until I finished college, and even then I didn't intend to make it a permanent arrangement. It just worked out that way."

"Why?" David asked.

She responded with candor. "I saw the children in the Ethiopia camps during a tour with my dad about five years ago. I couldn't forget their faces or their vulnerability, so I decided to pitch in and help. It felt like the right decision when I made it, and my feelings haven't changed."

"Even now?"

He heard the sigh that escaped her as she considered his question. He sensed her response to her question, but he wanted the satisfaction of hearing her say the words that would confirm his initial estimation of her character.

"Even now," she answered.

"I like you, Emma Hamilton. You've got grit."

"I don't know about having grit, but I like you too."

"I don't understand why the authorities picked you up. It's obvious you're no threat to the government."

"I was checking the status of one of our camps when my driver told me he had a personal emergency. He promised to return in plenty of time to take me to the airport for my flight home. I was so busy at the last camp I visited that I didn't think anything about his absence until I discovered that he'd stolen my travel documents, my airline tickets, and nearly all my money."

"And then?" he prompted.

"I decided to return to the capital city when I finished my report. I have a friend who works for the Canadian embassy. I knew she'd be willing to help me secure new travel papers and loan me the money for an airline ticket. I knew, too, that I'd need assistance acquiring a temporary U.S. passport. I was only a few blocks from her place when I was detained by the secret police." She sighed. "Now, we're neighbors."

"They'll realize their mistake," he automatically assured her, although as soon as the words left his mouth, he hoped he wasn't giving her false hope.

"I don't know if I share your optimism, David. No one would listen to me, and no one seemed inclined or willing to try to verify my claims."

He didn't feel capable of further encouragement so he refrained from voicing emotions he knew he couldn't fake.

"Tell me about your family," Emma urged. "I'm tired of talking about myself."

"You must be tired, period," he observed.

"I'm not the only one who needs to share, David."

"Playing shrink, Emma?"

"Just trying to be a friend," she chided, but the gentleness of her voice softened the impact.

"Thanks," he said, his voice roughened by a sudden onslaught of emotional hunger. "I guess I do need one just about now."

"Tell me about life in Montana," she encouraged.

"I grew up on a ranch."

"Now, why doesn't that surprise me?"

He smiled, his pride in his heritage surfacing. "I

don't get home that often anymore, but I'll end up there one of these days."

"After the Marine Corps?"

"Probably. I'm a partner in the ranch, but my first priority is aviation," he told her as he warmed to the subject. "It always has been, and I suspect it will be for a long time to come."

"I take it your family's still in Montana."

"My dad passed away during my first year in the Corps. Mom stayed on at the ranch until my younger sister married. Her husband runs the place now."

"I'm surprised your mother was willing to leave her home."

"She's a teacher, and it's more convenient for her to live in town, especially when winter sets in. She also wanted to make sure that Jenny and Zach had the privacy they needed for a good start to their marriage. They've got three kids now, and Mom apparently spends a lot of her weekends with them."

"She sounds like a terrific person."

He nodded, glimpsing members of his family through Emma's eyes. "I've always thought so. Mom was my strongest ally when I was trying to get Dad to understand that I wanted a career in aviation. She has a gift for helping people nurture their dreams. I was too damned determined at the time to really understand his disappointment that I had no intention of following in his footsteps. Mom wound up playing referee. I finally realized that her efforts made it possible for me to reconcile with my father before his death. I really owe her a major debt when it comes down to safeguarding important family relationships."

"Flying means everything to you, doesn't it?"

"I honestly can't imagine doing anything else, at least not at this point in my life."

"I understand what you're saying, David. I feel the same way about my work with Child Feed." She hesitated a moment before admitting, "I've been accused of not making time for a real life by some of my friends. One person in particular told me I was obsessed. I don't know. Perhaps he's right."

"Are *you* happy with your choices, Emma?"

"Very happy."

"Then forget what anyone else thinks. You won't go wrong if you keep trusting your instincts."

"That's good advice."

He laughed at the surprise he heard in her voice. "Why so shocked?"

"My dad said the same thing to me not long ago."

"Well, there you have it. Two intelligent males giving you sage guidance. Can't do any better than that, can you?"

"I suspect I could have." Self-incrimination underscored her remark.

"How's that?" he asked.

"David, think about it. I trusted my instincts and wound up in here."

"You took a calculated risk. Unfortunately you had no way of knowing all the potential ramifications of your actions, so don't beat yourself up over it," he instructed sharply. "Think of this situation as a classic example of an accident of fate. Pure and simple. Trust me, I've had plenty of time to come to that conclusion. As my buddy Dev MacKenzie always said, 'No one ever promised you a rose garden.'"

"That's a quaint perspective."

"No, babe, that's life, and this is the thorny part."

David closed his eyes against the darkness, his mood suddenly melancholy. He regretted that he'd allowed himself to inject such a cynical note into his conversation with Emma. He wanted to help her adjust, but he also longed for a respite from the steady, aching need that made him hungry for human contact and a thousand other things he knew he couldn't have.

"I wish we could be face-to-face when we talk to each other," she said after several moments of silence. "I'd feel better if I could see you."

"We can always try digging through the wall and meeting in the middle. It'd be a fascinating way to pass the time."

She ignored his stinging sarcasm. "Why don't we?"

"Forget it, Emma. I've tried and failed. This building may be old, but it's sturdy. It'll take a bomb blast to open up these walls."

David stiffened suddenly, and his eyes snapped open. A means of physical contact *did* exist. He just hadn't thought of it until now. Not surprising, he realized, because until Emma, he'd been the sole occupant of the cellblock.

He'd moved to a corner at the front of his cell. "We may not be able to see each other, Emma, but we're going to hold hands," he vowed as he slid his arm through the bars, angled his body into a position that offered little physical comfort, and then slid his hand along the wall that separated him from Emma. He intended to touch her and find out for himself if her skin was as soft as he'd imagined.

"What did you just say?"

"You heard me."

"I don't do magic tricks, David."

"We don't need magic. I'm just sorry I didn't think of this sooner, but we can make it happen if you're willing to meet me halfway."

"You aren't making any sense. We aren't capable of walking through walls."

"Of course I'm making sense," he disagreed. "Where are you standing right now?"

"Near the front of my cell."

"Good. Head to the bars and move toward me."

Silent for several moments, Emma announced, "I've decided to humor you, David."

"Just do as I tell you, all right?"

He listened carefully to her footsteps as she followed his instructions. When she stopped, he said, "Lift your hand until it's level with your shoulder. Once you've done that, find the gap between the bars closest to the wall and work your arm through. Then, extend your arm so that it's parallel to the wall."

"I'm working my arm through now."

"Be careful," he cautioned. "Sections of the wall are really jagged. You can't afford to cut yourself. A minor infection in this place could end up killing you."

"Nice thought," she muttered. "I'm in position. Now what?"

He reached for her but touched only grime-covered masonry. He frowned for a moment, then asked, "How tall are you, Emma?"

"Exactly five feet, four inches."

"Hold still. We're going to find out the true width of this damn wall." He slowly lowered his outstretched hand. An odd noise caught his attention, and he froze. "Did you hear something, Emma?"

"All I can hear is my heartbeat. It's absolutely deafening."

He smiled at the conspiratorial quality of her whispered reply. "That's not surprising. I can hear mine too."

"What happens next?"

He answered her question by stroking his callused fingertips across the knuckles of her hand. "This happens next," he said quietly.

"David?" she breathed in disbelief.

"Yeah, babe. It's me."

She laughed. He did, too, but the sound stalled abruptly in his throat and turned to a nearly silent moan of naked longing as he closed his large hand over the warmth of her smaller one.

Three

Emma didn't try to fight the tears that spilled from her eyes. Sagging back against the bars of her cell, she wept silently and savored the security and reassurance she found in David's touch.

"Feel better?" he asked several minutes later.

Swallowing her tears, she managed a faint yes.

He squeezed her hand. "Emma, don't cry. There's no need, at least not now."

"I know." She drew a shuddery breath. "I didn't mean to get all soggy on you, but I've been so frightened."

"With good reason," he reminded her. "You aren't alone, babe, so hang on to me for as long as you need."

"What did I tell you about that 'babe' stuff?" she groused.

He chuckled. She wiped at the tears streaming down her cheeks with her free hand, then held her breath when he began a slow exploration of each one of her fingers. He paused at the tips to run his thumb along the edge of her short trimmed nails before he deliberately trailed his fingertips across the back of her hand.

Emma tumbled into the rainbow of sensations that shimmered just below the surface of her skin. It stunned and delighted her, creating an acute yearning for more.

She suddenly knew that as a lover, David would be exquisitely thorough. That thought brought her up short, and she decided that hunger and fear must be making her light-headed and fanciful. "The woman in your life must adore it when you touch her."

His fingers stilled, and she grappled with her own shock and embarrassment. "There isn't a woman in my life, unless of course you're counting yourself."

"I've always thought that the sensitivity a man shows with his hands reveals his true nature." She laughed, the sound pitched high enough to betray her frayed nerves. "I'm saying things right now that I've never said to anyone before. I must be going a little crazy."

"Standing in the dark in a prison cell on the wrong side of the world tends to change the rules, doesn't it?"

She felt seduced anew by his low voice. "Then I guess that I can admit that I like your voice too. It's very sensual." The darkness had made her braver than usual. Perhaps brazen. Probably foolhardy, she concluded on a silent groan.

"You're easy to touch, Emma. Your skin reminds me of satin. So smooth and so incredibly soft."

Stunned by the awe she heard in his voice, she trembled beneath his gentle stroking, but she didn't pull away. She loved the warmth and substance conveyed by his fingertips. Convinced that he possessed a deeply sensual nature, she silently basked in the fantasies he provoked.

"Do you play the piano?" he eventually asked.

She felt as though he'd just asked her if she would consider making love with him. He had that kind of a voice, she realized. Seductive to the point of making her witless. So erotic that he also made her acutely aware of her very limited experience with men.

"Emma?"

"Did your cell come with a crystal ball?"

Instead of answering her right away, David slowly trailed a fingertip along the inside curve of her thumb. He lingered at the plump base, his touch light but incredibly provocative. Emma shivered in response.

"You've got the finger spread of a pianist. My mother and sister both play," he continued. "They insist that the hands determine success or failure at the piano, especially for a woman."

"I'm not very good at it."

"I suspect that you're very good at everything you do."

Shaken by his suggestive tone, she felt her heart lurch in her chest. Her only lover, a man relegated to her past, had rarely praised or complimented her. If anything, he'd found fault with everything she did or dreamed of doing, especially when it concerned Child Feed. "Hardly," she finally murmured.

David slid his fingertips up to her wrist. Emma held her breath and waited for his shock when he discovered her madly hammering pulse.

"Since I've been in here, I've wondered over and over if I'd ever touch a woman again." He loosely circled her wrist with his fingers. "You're so delicate and fine-boned, the least amount of pressure could damage you beyond repair."

She laughed softly, thinking of the heavy luggage she routinely hauled around the world.

"What's so funny?"

"I'm a lot tougher than you can imagine."

"Are you trying to tell me you eat nails for breakfast and then lift five-hundred-pound weights just for the hell of it?"

"Not exactly, but I'm certainly no cream puff." She purposely shifted the conversation back to David. How else would she be able to satisfy her growing curiosity about him and retrieve herself from the sensual pool she was drowning in? "You aren't a small man, are you?"

He chuckled. "Hardly. I was a linebacker in college. My coach claimed I had what it takes to turn pro, but it wasn't what I wanted."

"I'm a Charger fan."

"Amazing! A woman who actually likes football."

She grinned. "Sam calls me a salmon. He thinks

it's unnatural for a woman to appreciate contact sports."

"I think Sam's a tad cynical where you're concerned."

Emma laughed aloud. "Sam's plagued with an incredible intellect, but he has to work at not being sexist. He's not really that bad, just annoyingly overprotective."

"Maybe he loves you and doesn't want to see you hurt."

Something about his gentle tone of voice told Emma that David's thoughts had returned to his family in Montana. "You're thinking about your sister, aren't you?"

"Bingo!"

Sensitive to the emotion she heard in that single word, Emma quickly reverted to their original topic. "From what I know about linebackers, they're broad across the shoulders, narrow at the hip, and they usually stand well over six feet tall, so how do you manage to fit into the cockpit of one of those little jets?"

"Snugly," he teased good-naturedly. "Since you're obviously lusting after my bod, are there any other vital statistics you'd like to know about?"

"Your ego's totally out of control, David Winslow, but I still like your hands."

"They're really pretty beat-up, especially after all those years of working on the ranch and then playing ball."

"They might be beat-up, but they're the hands of a man who would never use his physical superiority against a woman," she said firmly.

"An observation like that makes me think that you've seen too much of the cruelty in our world, Emma Hamilton."

She responded candidly to his sober observation. "I've seen enough to know that the work I do is valuable, and I've experienced enough to know what I want and what I won't tolerate in my private life."

His fingertips came to rest on the underside of her wrist. Her pulse accelerated even more. Emma froze, and images flooded her mind. His fingers on her body, his hands smoothing down her back to her hips, molding her lower body to his loins before he brought his hands forward and finally filled them with the weight of her aching breasts. A coil of desire tightened deep inside her. Her skin tingled. Although she knew the absurdity of her fantasies, she felt a riot of sensation explode in her bloodstream.

"Emma . . ."

She registered his surprise in the stark way he said her name and in the hesitation of his callused fingertips the second he encountered her racing pulse. Embarrassed and certain he considered her response to him silly, she waited for him to pull away. He shocked her by grasping her wrist even more securely.

"Babe?"

"Yes?" she whispered breathlessly. She felt his tender strength whisper over her skin like hot currents of tropical air.

"Do I make you nervous?"

Startled more by the seductive tone of his low voice than by his actual question, she insisted, "Not at all. Being in jail, however, isn't exactly a tranquil experience."

"Whatever you say."

Turning her hand, she laced their fingers together. "Please don't let go of me, David."

His grip tightened, warmth flowing from his fingers to hers. "I don't intend to, but I have to admit that your grip shoots my cream-puff theory all to hell."

She grinned, some of her tension easing. "I think I like the sound of that."

"I have a confession to make."

"Be my guest," she quipped, anxious to divert his attention away from her racing pulse.

"Touching you is incredibly arousing."

Emma drew in a stunned breath. "But all we're doing is holding hands."

"I know. Shocking, isn't it?"

"You've been alone for a long time, David."

He exhaled so heavily that he sounded as if he was groaning. "It's more than that."

"How can you be so certain?"

"Not just any woman would suit me," he insisted. "I'm more discriminating than you seem to think."

"I wasn't trying to insult you, but two months of enforced celibacy can't be easy on a man, especially a man like you."

"A man like me?" he echoed, obviously startled and offended.

Emma grappled with her own fluctuating emotions and the desire that was still flirting with her senses. "David, I'm not numb. Nor am I stupid. You're obviously a very sensual man."

"I'm not into sexual conquests."

"Let's change the subject. This conversation is academic anyway."

"Is it?" he asked in a hushed tone of voice. "You may not want to believe it, but we both know there's something happening between us, and it's nothing so mundane as simple biological urges. I'm drawn to you, babe. I'm not sure why or if I even like the feeling, and I don't understand it any more than you do."

She tried to tug free of his fierce hold, but she quickly discovered that he didn't intend to relinquish her hand. "We need to concentrate on the basics. You know as well as I do that anything else is impossible."

"I still want you, Emma. I don't think that's going to change."

She trembled. "Maybe holding hands isn't such a good idea after all." She tried again to ease her hand from his grasp, but she failed.

"Please, don't pull away from me. I need . . . I need you right now. There's been precious little goodness in my life in recent years, not to mention the last few months."

She ached to reassure him when she heard the raw emotion of his strained voice, but she still felt haunted by the accusations of inadequacy she'd endured from her first and only lover. She gathered her courage and admitted, "I've never been very good at meeting other people's expectations."

"I don't have any real expectations where you're concerned, only fantasies," he said tiredly. "Just be yourself, Emma. Nothing more, nothing less. I already like you too much to try to force you into being someone or something you aren't."

"Are you sure you can accept me as I am and not as you'd like me to be?" She waited for his reply, struggling for calmness and for an understanding of the chemistry flowing between them.

"Very sure."

Still uncertain despite his assurance, Emma waffled about how to respond, but her honesty triumphed. "David, I know there's more between us than our proximity to each other. It's just that a lot's happened to me in a very short time. I haven't come to terms with it all yet."

"Believe it or not, I really do understand what you're going through."

"I know you do. That's why I trust you to respect my feelings."

She felt him shift his upper body, and his fingers slid across her palm. Sensation flitted through her nerve endings once again. She fell silent, her thoughts drifting in a bewildering maze until David asked an unexpected question.

"Did they take your jewelry?"

Startled, Emma jerked back to reality. "What jewelry?"

"Your watch, rings, necklace, earrings, that kind of thing."

"Just my watch."

His soft chuckle reached her. "You're going to make me ask, aren't you?"

"Ask what, David?"

"Are you engaged? Or worse, married?"

"Oh, no. Neither. Who in the world would put up with my schedule?" She hesitated, stumbling over the fact that she hadn't even considered the possibility that David might be involved in a relationship. "Are you? Married, I mean."

"I was until a couple of years ago. She didn't like the life-style."

"Children?"

"None. You?"

"Not yet, but I want them very much."

"Me, too, but I haven't found a woman who's willing to tolerate the constant transiency of military life. It's not an easy way to live."

"I don't imagine it is," she mused, although she thought that a woman, or a man, could tolerate just about anything under the right circumstances. She also doubted that life with a sensual, compassionate, and intelligent man like David would be at all difficult. "How old are you?" she suddenly asked.

"Thirty-five . . . last week."

"We'll have a party when we get out of here," Emma promised.

More relaxed now, he chuckled softly. She sensed his surprise at her offer. She also appreciated the fact that he didn't question her motives.

Growing inside her, she realized, was a profound need to bring pleasure into the life of David Winslow, but it was too new and far too disconcerting to share.

Other than her family and the children served by Child Feed, Emma rarely invested herself in other people's lives. There simply wasn't time. A fluke of fate, however, had altered her entire world, shrinking it in some respects, expanding it in others.

David moved unexpectedly, and Emma felt his secure clasp on her hand loosen. Suddenly panicked, she grabbed for him before they lost contact altogether.

"Sorry. Just trying to get more comfortable."

She took a breath and willed her heartbeat to slow.

"Emma?"

"I'm all right."

"You're sure?"

"Yes," she whispered.

"I didn't mean to pull away or scare you, but I've got a cramp in my shoulder."

"Then maybe we should . . ."

"We'll have to fairly soon," he cautioned.

"Just warn me before you let go."

"You've got a deal, babe."

She relaxed when she heard the teasing in his comment. "You're hopeless."

"So I've been told."

"I guess I'm stuck with that 'babe' stuff, aren't I?"

"It'll be our secret."

She warmed to the intimacy of his low voice. "Promise?"

"Absolutely."

"Then I'll try not to cringe every time you use that abominable word, although it makes me think of Paul Bunyan's ox."

"I suspect you're prettier, and I know you're a hell of a lot smaller."

"I certainly hope so!"

"I've been wondering what you look like," he confessed.

She shrugged. "Pretty average, I guess."

"Define average."

"Well, you already know that I'm five-four and have dark hair."

"It's long, isn't it?" he asked, his question a sighing sound of seduction.

"Almost down to my waist. For the sake of convenience I usually braid it."

"And your eyes?" he prompted.

"Blue," she answered. "I inherited my dad's Irish complexion. Mom's northern Italian, and I share her penchant for good food. As a result, I'm always dieting."

"I like a woman with meat on her bones."

"My hips thank you," she said with a giggle.

"You sound perfect."

"Far from it, although every woman wants to be viewed that way."

"You also sound healthy and just as I imagined you'd look. Most women starve themselves and assume men enjoy making love to scarecrows."

She laughed. "I'll never have to worry about that." David suddenly tightened his fingers. "Your arm's really bothering you, isn't it?"

"I'm afraid so."

The regret she heard in his voice soothed her. "Maybe we should both try to get some rest now."

David squeezed her hand before drawing away his fingers. Emma kept her arm extended for a moment, reluctant to be separated from him.

"Are you all right?" she asked.

"I will be. I guess a dislocated shoulder takes awhile to heal."

"You should've told me."

"I was fine until a couple of minutes ago."

She finally withdrew her arm, moved out of the cramped corner, and leaned against the wall. She bowed her head and closed her eyes, sadness and a renewed sense of isolation creeping into her heart as she listened to David's pacing in the adjacent cell.

"I'm sorry, Emma."

Pushing her long hair away from her face, she straightened and hurried to the bars at the front of her cell. She wished she could ease his pain, just as much as she wished that she could walk straight into his arms and remain there forever. Holding hands had reassured her, but it had also aroused more profound needs.

"Don't apologize, David. It's really okay. I'm going to get some sleep. You've been wonderful and very patient."

"You make it easy, babe."

"Sleep well."

"You too."

Emma retrieved her wool cape from the pallet, wrapped it around herself, and sank to the floor. Using her tote bag as a pillow, she curled into a tight circle and closed her eyes. She conjured up the image of a large, ruggedly attractive man who possessed a ready wit, a deep reservoir of compassion, a remarkably sensual voice, and the instinctive ability to make her feel secure.

With David Winslow strolling the landscape of her thoughts, Emma soon drifted off to sleep.

Four

As she sat on the pallet in her cell and stroked a brush through her hair, Emma reflected on the stillness of the predawn hour. She had been in jail just over a week and had come to cherish this particular time of day because of its peacefulness.

Those few hours gave her a reprieve from the now familiar sound of air-raid sirens, exploding bombs, and antiaircraft fire, the cries of prisoners undergoing interrogation, and the intermittent rifle fire that echoed in the courtyard adjacent to the cell block.

Although often frightened, Emma realized that she'd discovered within herself the courage to hope for freedom and the strength to face each day. She periodically doubted David's assurances that she alone would determine how she handled imprisonment, because she thought of him as the source of her optimism.

Emma heard David stir in the adjoining cell, but

she remained silent and concentrated on braiding her hair. She then continued her morning routine by dipping a small section of the hem of her blouse into the inch of water remaining in her battered tin cup.

As she dabbed at her face and neck with the damp fabric, she longed for a luxurious soak in a tub filled with hot water and scented bubbles. The simple pleasures she'd always taken for granted, such as brushing her teeth and wearing clean clothes each day, had become a fantasy.

Emma welcomed the familiar sound of David's footsteps. After shedding her cape, she, too, paced her small cell. She walked for over an hour, swinging her arms vigorously as she adjusted her steps to his long-legged stride. Her western-style boots and his heavy leather flight boots quickly synchronized and gave the impression that only one person moved briskly back and forth across the cement floor.

Invigorated by the exercise, she returned to her pallet. She picked up her tote bag and searched for her notepad and pen. Somehow they had worked their way down to the bottom, and pawing past a soiled San Diego State University T-shirt, Emma encountered a pair of rolled socks.

Puzzled by the sharp edge she felt through the thick cotton, she fingered the socks. Hope sparked inside her. She hurriedly upended her tote bag, spilling the contents onto her lap. With disbelief and pleasure, Emma smiled at the foil-wrapped package peeking from the end of the rolled socks.

"Chocolate," she murmured. She handled the confection reverently as if it were a nugget of gold.

"I found a candy bar!" she exclaimed once she convinced herself that she wasn't hallucinating. Scrambling to her feet, Emma raced to the corner of her cell. "Did you hear me, David?"

"I'm not deaf."

Her smile faltered, but she refused to let his terse reply rob her of the joy of her discovery. She knew he expected her to observe their rule of silence during the early-morning hours, but Emma couldn't remain quiet. "It's still wrapped in foil, and it's in perfect condition. I can't believe I missed it. Nor can I believe that the guards missed it."

"I told you those guys were inept. I still have my watch. They overlooked it when they searched me."

"We'll share it, David."

"I don't like chocolate, so just eat the damn thing and shut up."

Startled, she fell silent, but comprehension dawned on her a few seconds later. She knew David well enough now to understand the motive behind his lie. She probably knew him as well as she knew herself. They had progressed from strangers trapped by dangerous circumstances to intimates who shared their thoughts, dreams, fears, and desires without a moment of hesitation.

Emma caught her breath as tears filled her eyes. Only David would pretend to hate something that he thought she needed. Only David would put her needs before his own.

She cleared her throat and straightened her spine. "Quit being a hero. It isn't necessary. There's plenty here for both of us, so stick out your hand. We're sharing this little treasure. I won't have it any other way."

"You need the energy, babe," he told her, his voice as rough as a stretch of gravel road.

"And you don't?" she asked, trying to keep from betraying the complex feelings he inspired in her. Feelings she kept locked in her heart for fear of becoming an even greater burden to him. Feelings that made her realize that she hovered on the brink of falling in love with him.

He exhaled heavily. "I'll get by. Give me a break, Emma, and just eat it."

"I refuse to take one bite of this chocolate bar if we don't share it."

"You're getting on my nerves, Hamilton."

"And you're behaving like a Montana mule, Winslow," she informed him. "Stop it and get over here so I can give you your half. If you don't cooperate, I'll give it to one of the guards."

He muttered a harsh expletive. Emma ignored it and waited for the sound of his footsteps. She heard instead the desert wind whistling in the eaves above the small barred window at the top of the rear wall of her cell. She felt her patience with him stretch to the limit.

"I'm putting you on notice as of right now, David Winslow. If you don't meet me at the wall, then I'll be forced to toss this candy bar in your direction and hope you can reach it. You should know, though, that I don't pitch worth a damn."

David moved to the corner of his cell, the briskness of his footsteps an obvious indication of his annoyance with her. "Your Italian is showing, babe."

"So's my Irish," she countered sharply. "Most sane men wouldn't willingly mess with such a volatile combination." Then she gentled her tone. "Don't fight me on this, David. You can't possibly win once I've set my mind on something."

"God save me from temperamental women."

Emma smiled, aware that his good humor had returned. Dividing the chocolate bar in half, she tucked her piece into the breast pocket of her blouse. After wedging herself into the now familiar corner of her cell, she slipped her arm through the bars and along the wall. She encountered empty space. "David, get your hand over here."

"You're getting bossy in your old age, Hamilton."

"So sue me."

Emma felt David's fingertips brush across her skin. When he cupped the back of her hand, the sureness of his touch reached inside her soul. She heard a heavy sigh escape him and felt the sting of tears in her eyes. How she longed to press herself against his sturdy body and feel the warmth of his embrace.

"I've missed you," he said gruffly. "Maybe we should revise our hand-holding schedule. An hour each morning added to our afternoon and evening sessions."

She pressed the back of her hand against his palm, burrowing against him as best she could as she savored his touch. "Only if your shoulder can take it."

"I can handle anything if it means I can touch you, babe."

Emma opened her mouth, but her reply died the instant she heard the heavy metal door at the end of the cell block hallway slam open. She inhaled sharply in panic and nearly lost her grip on David's half of the candy.

"Get back, Emma. Now!"

Emma jerked backward, wincing when she scraped her shoulder against the wall's rough surface, and dashed into the rear of her cell.

Her heart raced. She knew that the guards rarely bothered with prisoners this early in the morning. Counting at least four sets of footsteps, she pressed herself against the wall and held her breath.

Four instead of one. She shuddered, fear prompting hot and cold flashes throughout her body as her heartbeat echoed in her ears. Four guards instead of one. Why? she wondered frantically, although she feared that she already knew the answer.

The armed men bypassed her cell, then stopped in front of David's. She stood there, shaken down to her toes as the guards dragged open his cell door. One of them barked an order. Emma strained to hear David's reply but heard only silence—a measure of his stubbornness.

Suddenly a scuffle erupted in his cell. David mustn't know she was afraid, she cautioned herself as she listened in horror. When she heard his groan of pain and the angry words he shouted at the guards, she moaned, then clapped a hand over her mouth.

Her sixth sense told her that he would try to make them forget that she occupied the adjacent cell. "David?" she whispered. She needed to tell him not to try to protect her, but how? Stymied by her fear that she might cause him more harm, she kept silent.

One of the guards shouted in Arabic. David exploded, his response a string of earthy curses that revealed his rage.

Emma surged forward and threw herself against the bars of her cell, heedless of the risk to herself. Clinging to the bars, she struggled to see beyond the uniformed men who blocked her view.

One of the guards turned suddenly and pointed his rifle at her. Emma hurriedly backed away. She tripped over the edge of her pallet, lost her footing, and landed in a sprawl on the cement floor.

Breathing raggedly, she brought herself up to her knees just in time to catch a glimpse of David as he was hauled from his cell. She registered the dark mahogany of his thick hair, the fury darkening his shadowed hazel eyes, and the fierce expression on his rugged face. Defiance made his broad-shouldered, narrow-hipped body rigid with tension and fury. She screamed his name before she could stop herself.

"Beat them at their own game, babe," he urged despite the blood trailing from the side of his mouth.

Emma jammed her fist against her lips to keep from calling out to him a second time. One of the guards silenced David with a punch to his midsection. He gasped and slumped forward, but the guards kept him from sliding to the floor.

She watched in horror as they dragged him away, and flinched when the cell block door finally crashed shut.

Still huddled on the floor, she clutched David's half of the chocolate bar to her chest. Tears streamed down her cheeks. She lost track of time, frozen in place by apprehension.

When she found the strength to move, she forced herself to her feet and paced. She tried to comfort herself by reliving every moment of her time with David. She repeatedly replayed their many conversations through her mind, but the haunting sounds of prison life, the cries of prisoners, and the sound of rifle shots tortured her.

By mid-afternoon Emma feared she might never see David again. Bowing her head as she leaned against the cell wall, she summoned what remained of her strength and prayed that the man who'd captured her heart would return to her. She also made a silent vow that she would employ her wits and all that David had taught her in order to ensure her own survival. She already knew that he would remain in her thoughts and in her heart for the rest of her life.

Wrapped in her cape, Emma finally collapsed across her pallet shortly after dark.

"Can you hear me, David?"

Seated cross-legged on his pallet, David retreated from the concern he heard in her voice. The guards had thrown him back in his cell after long hours of having his back, arms, and legs beaten with rubber hoses, and for nearly four days since then he refused to speak, refused to burden Emma with the cruelty he'd endured.

"David?"

Shutting out the sound of her voice, he pressed the back of his head against rough stone and mortar, kept his hands at his sides, and closed his eyes, but he couldn't empty his mind or control the shaking of his body.

"Just tell me you're all right," Emma pleaded. "I don't expect conversation, just a hint that you can hear me."

He inhaled deeply to try to calm himself. He failed. Instead he experienced a renewal of his rage.

"David," she whispered. "Let me help you. You've done so much for me. It's my turn now."

"No," he managed through gritted teeth.

"I can feel you drifting away from me. David, please. I can't let that happen. You're a part of me. You always will be."

He wrapped his arms around his aching ribs before lowering his forehead to his drawn-up knees. Self-pity assaulted him, and he shuddered as he forced himself to nurse back to life the fragile kernel of courage in his soul.

"I know it's hard for you to speak to me right now, but I want you to try. I just wish . . ."

Giving in to his need for the one person he

trusted and cared about, he groaned, "Wish . . . what?"

"I wish I could put my arms around you and hold you."

"Me . . . too," he admitted haltingly, then forced himself to continue—for Emma and for his own sanity, because he sensed that she was the only thing standing between him and madness. "Talk to me . . . babe. Need you . . . to help me . . . forget."

Emma didn't hesitate. "We need each other, David. We're a team. No one can change that." Tears filled her eyes, but she hastily brushed them away. "While you were gone, I imagined all kinds of terrible things happening to you. Some of them probably did, but I know you won't tell me. You still think I'm a total cream puff, don't you?"

"No! Don't . . . think that . . . at all."

"Well, even though you've tried to protect me from what's really going on in this place, my ears work and I have too vivid an imagination not to comprehend the reality of our situation."

She sighed, the sound audible in the uncharacteristic silence of the postmidnight hour. "You've shared your strength and your courage, David, sometimes at your own expense. You've also taught me valuable things about myself. I know you're probably reluctant to trust me or to let yourself lean on me right now, but I promise I won't fail you."

"Know that . . . already." Lifting his head, he peered at his calendar and wondered if he'd have the strength to make the sixty-eighth mark.

"I was afraid you wouldn't come back to me," she admitted. "I can't imagine being without you."

He forced himself to respond, despite the pounding in his skull. "Bad pennies . . . always turn up."

"You are *not* a bad penny. In fact I think you're . . ."

He frowned when she hesitated. "What?"

"I think you're very special."

He savored the gentle quality of her voice as it washed over him in comforting waves. "Not special. Just very dented."

"David, I'm so sorry."

A harsh laugh escaped him. "Me too. Talk about . . . something else." Gathering what remained of his strength, he hugged his middle and slowly straightened. An agony-filled moan escaped him, but he quickly ground his teeth together and resisted the pain lancing through his bruised ribs.

"I was thinking about home today," Emma said. "I miss my cottage."

"Nice place?"

"I think so. It was originally a free-standing, four-bay garage at a beachfront estate. The owner's heirs were from New England and didn't have any interest in maintaining or using the property, so they put it up for sale. It was in such terrible condition that I was able to acquire the garage and the lot at a reasonable price, which is pretty unusual in California. After making some rough sketches of a cottage, I took my ideas to an architect and then hired my uncle, the contractor, to do the actual remodeling." She hesitated. "Do you really want to hear all this?"

"Yes."

"All right, then. We started from scratch, and the end result was a two-bedroom cottage in a very contemporary design. It's spacious, wonderfully private, and it sits at the edge of a high bluff. I even have a rose garden along one side of the house."

"Good view?" he asked, determined to hold up his end of the conversation.

"The most spectacular view of the beach and the ocean in the world," she said enthusiastically. "It's the first thing I see each morning and the last thing I see each night before I go to bed. I really miss it when I'm away. I love starting my day with a walk on the beach just as the sun comes up. It's serene, despite the fact that we get a lot of tourists. It's as though there's an unspoken understanding that we all respect one another's need for privacy."

David felt a sudden ache in his loins as he pondered sharing nights with Emma and then waking up beside her each morning. He suspected that her cherished Pacific view would pale in comparison to her naked sensuality.

"Braggart," he finally accused in response to her rave review of her home, but he felt the same way about his Montana ranch.

"You're darn right. I can't wait for you to see it, David. It's really a slice of heaven." She paused for a moment before revealing, "I think about it whenever I'm frightened, especially if I wake up in the middle of the night and can't get back to sleep. You'll understand why when you visit me."

He felt his heart lurch. "I'm invited?"

"Where else would we have your birthday bash?"

"I feel old enough right now . . . to celebrate a hundred birthdays, babe."

"You're just a little . . . dented," she reminded him, using his word. "You'll feel better once you've had some rest, which you should try to get now."

"Hope so."

"Is anything broken?"

"I don't think so. I'm just bruised all over."

"Rubber hoses?"

He heard her horror, despite her attempt to conceal it. "Yes."

"You'll get better. I know you will. You're the strongest, most resilient man I've ever known," Emma insisted before a sob shattered her composure.

"No. A cream puff." Ravaged by her tortured emotions, he begged, "Don't cry."

"I'm not."

"My ears work too."

"David—"

"And talk to me when you're frightened," he ordered.

She laughed tearily. "You must be feeling better already. You almost sound like your old self. And for the record, *Major* Winslow, I do talk to you when I feel like I'm losing it. I'd go nuts if I didn't."

"You aren't alone, Emma. I'm not worth much at the moment, but I'm here for you."

"You're worth everything, and then some. Now, get some rest."

"I need to hear your voice. . . . I can't sleep yet."

"You're sure?"

"Talk to me," he said stubbornly. "I don't want to sleep."

"Would you like to hold hands for a while?"

He wanted nothing more than to feel her again, to stroke her satin-smooth skin and caress her long, slender fingers. But he knew it was impossible, and cursed how weak he felt. "Can't do it, babe. Sorry."

"Tomorrow?"

"You've got a date." He prayed he'd have the strength to move then.

"Do you ever have nightmares?" she asked softly.

Having already discovered that Emma never judged, she simply listened, he knew in his heart that revealing the truth to her would be the most natural thing in the world for him to do. "Sometimes," he conceded.

"Not fun, are they?"

"Don't ask questions. Just talk, Hamilton."

"Yes, sir!"

He grinned in the darkness of his cell. "I think I'll teach you . . . to salute."

"Every woman's secret fantasy, and you're going to make mine come true. Be still, my heart."

He laughed, then promptly groaned when his body protested the rapid rise and fall of his chest. "Don't make me laugh, Hamilton. And keep talking."

"I'm a great cook," she immediately confided.

"More comic relief, or are you telling the truth?"

"I'm serious. My girlfriends think I'm crazy to even admit it, but I'm very much at home in the kitchen. I cook to relax. Then I get to diet. It's a vicious cycle."

"Maybe you should've become a caterer."

"I didn't feel inclined to tempt fate and ruin my waistline at the same time, thank you very much."

David slowly shifted his legs forward and massaged the tops of his thighs as he listened to the sweet sound of Emma's voice. It steadily dulled the pain throbbing in his body and soothed his anger. She spoke for nearly two hours, rambling from subject to subject, regaling him with tales of her childhood.

David refused to remain idle while she talked, but he listened to each word, finding strength in her generous spirit. As he kneaded the muscles in his legs, arms, and shoulders, David silently vowed that his future would include Emma. He couldn't imagine finding happiness without her.

He nearly succumbed to light-headedness as he struggled to his feet. Trembling and breathing raggedly, he pressed his cheek to the cold wall, closed his eyes, and focused on the sound of Emma's voice.

Driven by his desire to feel the comfort of her

soothing touch, he brought himself under control. David moved awkwardly and slowly, each step an exercise in terror as the muscles of his body tremored in constant protest, but he finally managed to position himself in the corner of his cell.

He caught his breath and then carefully maneuvered his arm through the narrow space between the bars and cell wall. Drops of sweat covered his upper lip and soaked the back of his flight suit. He shuddered, but he refused to give in to his weakness.

Emma soon fell silent, her fatigue evident in the heavy sigh that escaped her.

"I'm at the wall, babe."

She scrambled up from her pallet and made her way to the corner of her cell. "Are you strong enough to be on your feet?"

"I'm shaky, but I'm standing," he assured her. "And I intend to remain that way come hell or high water." He heard an odd sound and feared that she was near tears again. "Please don't cry."

"I'm not," she insisted. She cleared her throat and straightened her spine. "I saved your chocolate bar. Shall I pass it to you? It might give you the energy you need, David."

Closing his eyes against the moisture unexpectedly filling them, he tried to speak but found he couldn't. Getting emotional over a candy bar wasn't exactly his style, and he felt like a fool.

"Tell me what you want," Emma urged softly a few moments later.

"I . . . I want you, babe. I need to touch you."

She immediately extended her hand. David felt the brush of her fingertips. He clasped her wrist before taking her slender hand in his.

Neither spoke as warmth, friendship, and love flowed between them. They remained physically and emotionally linked as the dawn emerged and the sun burst onto the horizon of the early-morning Middle Eastern sky.

Five

"I'd give anything to take a shower and wash my hair."

"Dream on, babe."

David's reply grated on Emma's already frayed nerves. Feeling completely out of sorts, she stomped back and forth in her cell. She heard David chuckle and nearly threw a temper tantrum.

"I can't stand being so filthy. It's making me crazy."

"Use your imagination," he suggested, "and pretend you're relaxing in an enormous hot tub filled with warm, bubbling water. It's the closest you're going to get to clean until we get out of this dump." David laughed. "It'll also give me something to fantasize about."

"That's not good enough," she protested.

"You don't have any other options," he reminded her gently. "Deprivation's the rule of thumb around here, but I'm not telling you anything you don't already know, am I?"

The compassion in his voice took the edge off her frustration. Emma stopped her restless pacing and returned to her pallet. She took deep, cleansing breaths and worked at calming herself.

"David, I'm sorry. I don't mean to be such an infant, but I don't know how much more of this I can stand. It's been two weeks, and no one's tried to rescue us. Surely my parents or Child Feed realize what's happened. Why isn't someone doing something?"

"We can only hope."

"I know," she whispered bleakly. "I know you're right."

"How about a book or a movie?" he asked a short while later. "It might help pass the time."

She slumped forward and rested her head in her hands. Although she knew he wouldn't force her to share memories of movies they'd seen or books they'd read, she called upon what remained of her dwindling good humor and forced herself to cooperate. She owed him that at the very least.

Emma lifted her head, squared her shoulders, and asked, "What's your pleasure, Major?"

"A sexy flick," he promptly replied.

She laughed, the first positive sound to emerge from her in several hours. "You're absolutely hopeless. How about an adventure or a mystery with a knockout heroine?"

"Since it's your turn, you make the decision."

She weighed her options before asking, "Do you remember Part Two of 'The Devastator' series?"

"Who could forget? Milos Bekenberger as a

muscle-bound cyborg, and Cara Stone as the pumped-up mother of a boy destined to save the planet. Everybody had great pecs in that movie, especially the kid's mother. She was dy-no-mite."

Emma groaned. "Talk about a one-track mind."

"You may be right," he agreed with the exact amount of leer in his voice to prompt another delighted laugh from her.

Feeling more relaxed, Emma began to recount the movie. What she couldn't remember, she made up by painstakingly describing what she did.

David periodically chimed in with both outrageously suggestive remarks and insightful comments about the film. Emma reclaimed her sense of humor as they talked, and David unknowingly soothed her restless emotions with the warmth and resonance of the low, gravel-rough voice she'd grown to love.

They lingered at the end, critiquing the pacing of the movie and the performances of the actors. And they agreed, as they frequently did, that filmgoers and readers preferred the validation of their belief that good will ultimately triumph over evil. Given their current situation, it was a philosophy they both needed to hold on to.

Emma took a sip of water from her tin cup to wet her mouth before she got to her feet and prowled her cell once more. She eventually came to a stop in the corner, hungry for physical contact with David but reluctant to impose her needs on him. Although he insisted that he'd completely recovered from the interrogation, she didn't believe him. She knew he tired easily.

"Babe?"

She gripped the iron bars of her cell. "Yes?"

"You all right?"

"I'll live."

He exhaled, the sound harsh in the quiet of the cell block. "That's not what I asked."

"Self-pity's a wretched idea, so don't get me started up again," she cautioned.

"Do you need me?"

A shiver of expectation rippled through Emma. She knew he was asking if she wanted to hold hands. Had he already guessed that she longed to share much more with him, that she yearned to walk straight into his arms and be held and made love to by him?

"Is your shoulder bothering you?"

"Not to worry. It's almost a hundred percent."

"But I do worry," she admitted as she positioned herself between the cell wall and the bars, and extended her arm. She immediately felt the secure clasp of David's large hand as it closed over hers. She sighed shakily, savoring his touch.

Her eyes fluttered closed. Slowly, surely, and with the silence of total concentration, he soothed and aroused her with the sensuality of his touch. Nudging her hand slightly to the left, he slid his fingers over the back of her hand, around the plump ridge of flesh at the base of her thumb, and into the center of her palm.

Emma held her breath while he traced expanding circles of sensation into her sensitive skin, sensations that sent her pulse racing and her blood pounding through her veins. She closed her hand, capturing his fingers. She gathered them together so that the tips rested in the middle of her cupped palm and slowly stroked the length of his fingers with the smooth edges of her nails. She stroked up and down . . . up and down . . . up and down . . . until he groaned. The primal sound stirred the very depths of her soul.

She felt his hand tremble, but David didn't pull away. A consuming shudder of arousal swept across her soul like a wild brushfire. She heard David's ragged exhalation and felt the tremors that shook his body.

Tingling warmth drifted across her palm, up her arm, and into her body. Biting her lip to smother a cry of need, Emma felt her breasts swell and her nipples tighten almost painfully.

Heat swirled inside her, and flames ignited deep within her, scorching her nerve endings and shattering what remained of her composure. Tears filled her eyes as she teetered between seductive torment and the emotional anguish of trying to deny her escalating desire for David.

Emma ached all over. Tears spilled from her eyes and trailed down her cheeks. "David . . ." she breathed, her voice riddled with desire and frustration and a hundred unvoiced emotions.

David fought his own battle for control. His breathing grew even more ragged. He laced their fingers together, but he said nothing. He couldn't.

Emma swallowed her tears. "Forgive me."

"Nothing . . . to forgive," he finally managed through gritted teeth. "You're the most volatile living thing I've ever touched, Emma Hamilton."

"Should I apologize?"

He laughed, but the sound ended on a low moan. He needed her so badly, his body screamed for release. "I wouldn't want you any other way, babe."

They held on to each other for several silent minutes. The call to prayers sounded over the loudspeaker in the adjacent courtyard, but neither Emma nor David moved.

"Were you telling me the truth before?" she asked softly.

David frowned. "The truth about what?"

"Your shoulder really is better?"

"It's fine, and the bruises are starting to fade. I'm not quite as colorful as I was a few days ago."

"And you aren't having any trouble walking or breathing?" she pressed, still concerned that he might try to protect her from the truth.

"No, *Doctor* Hamilton," he teased. "No trouble at all on that score."

"David, this is important. Those men could have caused severe internal damage of some kind."

"My ego and my pride took more of a beating, babe."

"I know," she murmured. "I just worry about you, and I can't see for myself that you're all right, so I ask a lot of boring questions that drive you nuts."

David hesitated for a moment. "It's my turn to ask a question."

"Go ahead."

"What would you say if I told you that I want to make love to you?"

"I feel as though you make love to me every time you touch my hand," she confessed once she found the courage to be completely honest with him.

"It kind of feels that way most of the time, doesn't it?"

Flushed and shaken once again, she whispered, "Very much."

"I want more, babe. So much more. You're all I think about." The tone of his voice intensified. "You don't think about me . . . that way?"

"I think about you *that way* almost all of the time," she blurted out.

Stunned, he admitted, "I didn't realize . . ."

"How could you not realize?"

"You seem reluctant to talk about it."

"Only because I'm afraid we won't have a chance to know each other intimately."

"Why, babe?"

She stared at the iron bars of her cell. "That's kind of obvious, isn't it?"

"That's not what I meant. Why do you want to make love with me?"

"Because I care about you." And because I love you, she realized with utter certainty.

"Have you ever been in love?" he asked, his voice hushed.

"Once," she answered, "or so I thought. Now I realize it was nothing more than an infatuation."

"When did it end?"

"A few years ago. He wasn't willing to understand that I needed more than my time with him to feel complete as a person."

"Selfish."

She nodded. "Yes, he was very selfish."

"Was he also the person who accused you of not having time for a real life?"

"You have a good memory," she remarked. "He made that comment while he was packing his things and moving out of our apartment. At the time I felt as though he'd plunged a knife into my heart, especially since I'd already given up so much of my work with Child Feed in order to spend more time with him. He didn't think I'd gone far enough. I guess he assumed that I should have been satisfied to devote my entire existence to him. When I refused, he walked out on me."

"The creep did you a favor," David muttered.

Emma smiled; he was right. "I realize that now, but I certainly didn't when I was first alone. I was too busy licking my wounds and feeling abandoned."

He slipped his fingers free and trailed the tips across the back of her hand before bringing them to rest against the delicate inner curve of her wrist. Her pulse speeded up.

"What do I make you feel?"

She felt seduced anew by the rough sensuality of his voice. "I wouldn't even know where to start."

He remained silent for a moment, then asked, "What did you mean when you said I was a part of you?"

Surprised by his question, Emma carefully considered her reply. Their situation was too uncertain for her not to be as candid as he.

"When the guards took you away," Emma began slowly, "I thought I'd never see you again. That's when I realized how connected I felt to you. You've imprinted yourself on my heart, David Winslow," she whispered as he closed his hand over her narrow wrist. "As a result you've become a permanent part of me."

"Maybe you're just suffering from some bizarre version of Stockholm syndrome. Has it occurred to you that you might not want any reminders, and that includes me, of this place once we're home?"

"That's absurd, David," she protested strongly. "You're definitely not my jailer. You are, however, my ally, my friend, and my most trusted confidant. Jailers don't hold hands with their prisoners, console them after nightmares, make them feel safe in an impossibly dangerous environment, try to protect them, or share their survival skills."

He laughed, but without humor. "You don't have too many other options for friendship at the moment."

She searched for the right words to tell him that he filled her heart with hope and joy and a desperate need to survive until they were free to explore their feelings for each other. But before she could speak, he admitted, "I want to be more than your friend and confidant. I want to be your lover."

"I want that too," she breathed, but her words were lost in the squeal of the cell block door as it swung open. "Oh, God, not again."

David gripped her wrist as footsteps sounded at the far end of the hallway. "Listen," he ordered.

"Listen to what?"

"Two sets of footsteps."

She concentrated on the sound. "They're moving more slowly than usual, aren't they?"

"Get away from the bars now. With a bit of luck, this might be the meal they neglected to bring us yesterday. If it's not, don't panic and don't let them see that you're afraid of them."

Emma quickly squeezed David's hand and then released it. Slipping out of her corner, she worked her way down to the shadows. Her heart thudded wildly against her ribs, her hands fisted at her sides, and her empty stomach growled at the prospect of a crust of bread and a bowl of watered-down soup.

Two young men wearing ill-fitting uniforms paused in front of Emma's cell. They peered at her, their curiosity evident. Although they carried weapons, neither one seemed inclined to wave them at her in a threatening manner, which was the custom of the other guards.

If anything, she realized with surprise, they seemed awkward and uncertain. One stepped forward and fumbled with the rusty lock of her cell door. He slid the door open, took her by the arm, and propelled her forward into the hallway.

"Emma? You okay?" David asked.

"So far," she answered, her eyes darting between the two youths. "I don't understand what's happening. Where are they taking me?"

"Stay calm," he urged. "Don't antagonize them."

She glanced backward and spotted David's powerful, white knuckled hands gripping the bars of his cell. "They're not as mean or as experienced as the other guards," she reassured him.

"You'll be all right, babe."

One of the young men clapped a hand over her mouth to silence her. Panicked, Emma jerked free and cried, "David! Don't forget me!"

"Never," he vowed. "Never!"

They hustled Emma out of the cellblock, kept walking, and a few minutes later shoved her through an open doorway. Emma stumbled forward as the door to the room closed behind her. She heard the lock being secured at the same time that she noticed the two women standing on either side of her. Both held deadly-looking handguns.

Backing away from them, Emma searched for an avenue of escape. But all she saw were sealed windows at the top of the tiled walls and an old-fashioned showerhead mounted on the far wall.

Emma retreated as the two women advanced on her. Even when she felt the wall against her spine, the women kept coming at her. She cringed when one of them reached out and tugged at the sleeve of her blouse before stepping aside and turning on the nearby showerhead. Her companion prodded Emma under the cold water with the unfriendly end of her weapon.

Emma decided against removing her clothes. Modesty, she knew, was stressed in the Middle East, especially among the women. She spotted a wedge of soap in a basket on the floor and reached for it.

She clumsily scrubbed at her clothes and her hair. One of the women yelled at her in Arabic and made emphatic motions with her weapon; the other pulled at her soggy clothing once again. Embarrassed, she nonetheless complied with their obvious expectation. Shedding her clothes, she kept her eyes shut and hurriedly washed herself while her face burned with humiliation and outrage.

Emma remained silent as the shower was turned off. Shivering, she gathered the pile of sodden garments at her feet, but it was snatched out of her hands.

After being motioned forward, Emma followed one of the women to a cabinet on the far side of the room. Once there, she was given a voluminous native black robe and veil. Although still wet, she dressed quickly. She retrieved her own clothes, and they escorted her to a deserted courtyard.

Emma stood between the women, who made themselves comfortable on wooden benches. Tucking her clothing under one arm, she removed the veil and finger-combed her long hair with her free hand. The light breeze and pleasant midday sun did nothing to ease the panic she felt.

Her thoughts repeatedly strayed to David. While she longed for an end to her imprisonment, she knew she would find little satisfaction in freedom if he remained in captivity. Surely their captors realized that if they released her, she wouldn't remain silent about David. If anything, she would shout his status and location to the world until they were reunited.

Emma thought that hours must have passed before the two women jumped into action once more. She watched in horror as they fashioned a leash with twine, but held her head high as they looped it around her wrists and then led her through a large kitchen. When an old man surreptitiously shoved two oranges into the folds of the wet clothing she carried, she nodded gratefully. She was locked in a storeroom and left alone to languish.

Emma sat on the floor and stared at the two oranges as time passed. She tried to imagine her future without David and saw nothing but an endless black void. And despite her hunger, she refused to eat even a small piece of the fresh fruit until she could share the unexpected treat with David.

Six

Don't forget me.

"As if I could ever forget you, Emma," David muttered to himself as he prowled his cell like a beast deprived of his mate.

Torn between his hope that her release had finally been secured and his fear that Emma was being subjected to a lengthy and cruel interrogation, he paced unceasingly for hours. Even when his common sense surfaced to protest the futility of his behavior, David ignored it and the aching in his muscles.

Guilt gnawed on his conscience. He wanted her out of harm's way, but he also selfishly craved her continued presence in the cell block. He loved her and he needed her, but he wanted her safe.

Exhaustion finally forced David to sit on his pallet. He stared at the floor watching the puddle of light from the window at the top of his cell slowly shrink.

Don't forget me.

Her words continued to echo in his mind. Exhaling raggedly, he leaned back, rested his head against the wall, and wondered once again how she could think that he'd ever forget her. He dreaded being without her, and he loathed not knowing what was happening to her. He'd feared for both his life and his sanity before her arrival.

She'd given him the gift of hope. He treasured her confidence and faith in him, although he doubted that he deserved them. He savored the vulnerability she revealed when they shared information about their lives, her tender way of viewing those she cared about, and the explosive attraction that sent desire shimmering through his body whenever they touched.

He desired her in the same way any healthy man desired the woman who aroused his passion and stirred his imagination, but he longed for her in numerous other ways too. She fed his soul with her sensitivity, made him laugh with silly jokes, eased his loneliness with her compassion, and she nurtured whatever courage he possessed with her belief in him.

Emma had helped him rediscover his ability to love. In the years since his divorce he'd closed himself off to all emotional involvement, but in just two weeks Emma had opened his heart and expanded his world. She'd become the center of both. Although he felt reluctant to speculate about what might happen between them in the future, he desperately wanted the freedom that would allow them to know each other as man and woman.

David closed his eyes to the darkness that finally engulfed his cell. He prayed that Emma wasn't simply clinging to him out of fear. He understood her need to feel safe, but his instincts told him not to discount the possibility that she wouldn't want or need him once they were free.

His emotions in disarray, he sought comfort in his thoughts and fantasies of Emma. Exhaustion finally claimed him, though, and he fell into a restless doze with an ethereal mental image of Emma walking naked out of a bank of swirling mist. Seconds later she stepped into his embrace, but when he closed his arms around her, she disappeared.

David Winslow moaned in his sleep.

The scrape of rusty metal as someone slid open the adjacent cell's barred door jolted David awake a few hours later. He remained seated on his pallet until the footsteps of the retreating guards faded and the hinges of the cell block door shrieked that it was closed.

David, immediately recognizing the distinctive sound of Emma's pacing, scrambled to his feet and raced to the corner of his cell.

"David?"

Several silent seconds passed as he dealt with his despair that she hadn't been released and his relief that she'd been returned to him. "You all right, babe?"

"I missed you, David."

He frowned at the flatness of her voice. His worry that she'd been cruelly handled by their captors increased. "Are you all right?" he asked again.

"I am now." She sighed softly, the sound one of enormous fatigue.

"What happened?" he pressed.

"I'm not sure."

"Emma, talk to me. Tell me what happened. I've been worried sick about you."

"Touch me, David. I need you to hold my hand more than anything right now."

He reached out and they connected. "What do I smell?" he asked, his senses alert to both the tremors of uncertainty in her voice and the scent drifting up from her skin.

"Soap. They let me bathe. I don't know why, though."

"Maybe they're getting ready to release you," he replied.

"I doubt it. I suspect the powers-that-be didn't want me to get too ripe, or maybe they didn't like my Western clothes. Who knows?"

"You don't sound like you care, babe."

"I only care about one thing," she admitted, her voice still ragged.

He closed his eyes and promised himself that he would proceed at her pace despite his clamoring need to whisk her through this crisis. "What's that?"

"Being with you."

David cautioned himself against reading too much into her comment. After all, who else did she have to turn to in this insane situation? Fingering the coarse fabric that fell across her wrist, he asked, "Did they take your clothes?"

"No, but they're wet from my shower. They gave me some other things to wear. I've gone native."

A disconcerting thought punctured his consciousness. "Were you alone when you washed up?"

"Not quite," she said with a shaky laugh. "There were two women. They had the most deadly-looking handguns I've ever seen." She paused, and David felt a violent shudder pass through her. "It was an embarrassing situation, but I guess I shouldn't be surprised that they didn't allow me any privacy."

"Enjoy being clean, babe. Forget the rest."

"I will . . . eventually."

"Did . . . were you interrogated?"

"No."

"Be thankful."

"I'm more thankful to be back with you. They locked me in a storeroom for hours and hours, and I was so afraid I'd never see you again. I won't leave here without you, David. I won't!"

His heart ached when he heard the rising terror in her voice, but he refused to lie to her. "You may not have a choice."

"I won't leave you. I can't." She started to weep. "I love you," she said through her tears.

I think I love you, too, he replied silently. But

how will you feel, he wondered, once we're free and it isn't just the two of us against the world? What happens then?

David ground his teeth together and tightened his grasp on her hand. He felt helpless and frustrated that he couldn't hold her and comfort her. "We need to talk about what you'll say to the authorities once you're released."

"Not now, David. I've brought you a present that won't wait."

She withdrew her hand, and when she extended it again, she deposited one of the oranges into his palm.

"How?" he asked in disbelief.

"An old man working in the prison kitchen. My guards led me past his work station at the end of a leash," she explained, the brittle edge in her voice revealing her fury at such demeaning treatment. "He tucked two oranges into the folds of my clothes as I walked past him."

David transferred the precious fruit to his free hand and then tucked the orange into the side pocket of his flight suit before reclaiming Emma's trembling fingers. The lump in his throat kept him from expressing his appreciation.

"They didn't hurt me, David. They just scared the daylights out of me. I'll be all right."

"You need some rest," he said, his voice grating roughly.

"I need you," she moaned.

David knew he had to make an effort to divert Emma from her thoughts. She was close to succumbing to a bout of self-pity. All too familiar with the consequences of such a negative state of mind, he crisply reminded her, "Once your clothes are dry, put them on beneath the robe they've given you. That way your teeth won't rattle when you get cold."

She giggled. "Yes, sir."

"We really do need to deal with the possibility that you'll be released first, Emma."

She tightened her grip on his hand. "There's nothing to discuss. I'll tell everyone exactly where you are. I know enough about the capital city to pinpoint our location on a map. Trust me, why don't you?"

"These people aren't fools. They'll move me."

"Then I'll have to get to the right people very quickly," she commented.

He heard her determination and found it strenghtening. "You won't let them forget me, will you?"

"Dumb question, Major Winslow."

Whatever control he thought he had over himself snapped. No longer willing or able to keep himself from revealing his emotions, he said, "I felt so alone when they took you away, babe."

"Oh, David, I understand. I thought I'd lose my mind when you were interrogated."

"I want you safe, but I don't want to lose you either."

"You won't lose me," she vowed.

He longed to believe her, but he feared the risk involved. He gently caressed the back of her hand before slipping his fingertips into the center of her palm, which he stroked until streamers of fire linked their bodies and their hearts. Emma grew breathless and trembly, and David hoped she would forget for a time the terror and humiliation she'd endured that day.

"What do you believe in, David?" she asked softly a little while later.

He candidly voiced his reply. "Us."

Emma smiled. "What else?"

"All the traditional things. Duty. Honor. Country. Freedom. My family."

"I'm glad you put us first."

"We are first in this situation."

She exhaled wistfully.

"Don't stop talking to me, babe. I haven't quite figured out how to read your mind, so I don't know what you're thinking right now."

"Take a wild guess," she suggested.

He laced their fingers together, his grip sure and strong and very possessive—as possessive as a lover's would be. "You're wondering what it'll be like when we make love."

Amazement in her voice, she asked, "How did you know?"

"I'm thinking along the same lines. So's my body."

"Painful, isn't it?" she observed wryly. "I ache all over."

David laughed, but the sound ended in a low groan. "Don't make it worse, babe."

"It'll be wonderful, won't it?"

"Intense. Very intense," he promised through gritted teeth as a fire raged inside him and brought to life the most male part of him. "You're a sensual woman, and you obviously like to touch and be touched."

"I've never responded to anyone in quite this way, David."

"Good. I don't want to share you."

"What kind of a lover are you?" she asked.

The timidity in her voice made David hesitate and carefully weigh his response. "Patient, I hope."

"And sensitive?"

"And very thorough," he promised. "I care what happens to my partner. My father once told me that putting a woman's pleasure first increased a man's satisfaction tenfold."

"You apparently agree."

"My old man may have been hard as nails some of the time, but he knew what he was talking about." Emma's silence prompted him to observe, "Turnabout's fair play. What kind of lover are you?"

She sighed and snugged her hand more securely against his. "Inexperienced. I've only been with one man, and he wasn't . . . well, he wasn't very patient with me."

Something stilled inside David. "He didn't abuse you, did he?"

"Oh, no. He just didn't have any patience. He always seemed preoccupied with his own satisfaction. I kind of felt as though I was just along for the ride. No pun intended." She paused. "This is a crazy conversation. I think I'm glad you can't see me right now."

"Are you blushing?"

"All over," she whispered.

Scalding rivers of sensation flowed through his bloodstream at her reply. His body grew as taut as piano wire, and his heart galloped like a racehorse on the home stretch. "I want you to enjoy what we share, babe."

"I'm certain I will."

David groaned silently at the erotic images flooding his mind. He lowered his forehead to the cold wall and struggled to cope with the desire surging hotly within his tense body. He failed. Completely.

"You don't mind that I'm not very experienced?"

"No," he gritted out.

"Then what's wrong? You sound awful."

"Nothing. Nothing at all. It's just that I have this fantasy in my head about us . . . together."

"Naked?" she whispered.

"Very naked."

"Breathless?"

"Absolutely."

"Passionate?"

"Emma." He stretched out her name until it seemed to contain a thousand syllables.

"You sound awful again."

"One of the hazards," he admitted ruefully, "of wanting you all the time." He felt a tremor shake her. "Your skin's on fire, and I'm on fire for you."

"All of me's on fire. All of me, every time I imagine the intimacy we'll share once we're free."

"We will. I promise you we will." Despite his body's crying need for fulfillment with Emma, he pushed his mind beyond the torture of fantasizing about what he couldn't have. The effort cost him and proved to be an excruciating second-by-second process. "Did anyone rough you up?"

"When?" she asked, obviously puzzled by his change of subject.

"When they took you away," he reminded her, his voice nearly as rigid as his body.

"I'd almost forgotten about that."

"Babe, you're tying me in knots with that dreamy tone of voice. Let's get back to reality before I die of wanting you."

"If you insist," she grumbled. "No one physically mistreated me. Other than the two women who supervised my shower and the old man who gave me the oranges, I didn't have contact with anyone else in the prison."

"You were lucky. At least you were kept away from the male guards."

"That's something, I suppose. But where I come from, bathing is a singular enterprise."

"Or with your lover," he suggested playfully when he heard her prissy tone.

"I've never done that kind of thing with a man."

"Would you like to?" he asked, his imagination kicking in and providing him with all kinds of seductive images.

"You could persuade me," she admitted shyly.

A rocket and grenade attack commenced a few miles from the prison, and an air-raid siren suddenly wailed in the distance. David tightly gripped Emma's hand. Both fell silent as the pinpoint of light at the far end of the hallway flickered and then died. Total darkness shrouded the cellblock.

"The bombing seems to get closer every night," Emma observed.

David nodded. "Maybe we'll luck out and the prison's administrative offices will wind up on the receiving end of an incoming rocket."

"That won't help us."

"Maybe not, but it sure would reward those bastards who tried to turn me into a chunk of raw hamburger."

Emma's hand jerked at the bitterness in his voice. "It'd be better if someone blew out the cell block wall."

"Only in our dreams, and only if you crave the idea of being blown up along with the building."

"It's a risk I'd take if I thought it meant getting out of here and making a run for freedom."

"I share your sentiments, babe, but I don't want you hurt."

"No more than I want you harmed, David, but the longer we remain here, the weaker we become. I've lost weight, as you predicted, and I know you've dropped at least twenty pounds, probably more."

"Closer to twenty-five," he conceded.

"We need an out. Some crazy political faction trying to undermine the government is our best hope."

David chuckled. "You'd made a great W.M."

She didn't recognize the term. "A what?"

"Woman Marine. You've got the grit. I also think that you're the strongest, sexiest woman I've ever known, whether or not you realize it. I'm glad we're on the same side."

"Thank you, I think." She paused. "Promise you won't laugh if I tell you a secret?"

"I'd never laugh at you, babe."

She admitted, "I say a prayer every single night that someone will blow out the cell block wall. And I keep my head covered with my shawl and curl my body into as tight a circle as I can manage. I generally fall asleep waiting for an explosion."

"Someday soon," he vowed, "I'll hold you all night long, and this entire experience will just be a bad memory."

"That's a promise I intend for you to keep, Major Winslow, but for the time being you should eat your orange. You need the vitamin C."

After gently snugging their laced fingers together one last time, they withdrew their hands and returned to their pallets. They continued to talk as they each savored the gift of a nameless old man who'd taken pity on them.

Forty-eight hours later the miracle they both constantly hoped for became a reality when a violent blast shattered the stillness of the night.

Stunned out of a sound sleep, Emma kept her cape over her head as she struggled to sit up. David shouted, "Incoming!" and a secondary blast filled her with terror.

Exploding grenades and rocket shells sent repeated shudders through the cell block walls, forcing Emma to gather her wits. Emma silently blessed Sam for dragging her along to countless war movies during their childhood. She knew what to do, she told herself as she ducked down and covered her head with her arms. Mortar dust sifted from the ceiling and the walls, filling the air with a gritty, siltlike debris.

Emma squinted up at the window of her cell. She saw strange flashes of light and heard the shriek of additional incoming rounds. The resultant explosions briefly deafened her and sent her sprawling across her pallet.

"Emma!"

"I'm all right, David," she gasped as she struggled to her knees.

"Whoever they are, these guys aren't too far away. And they obviously mean business."

"Do you think . . ." She lost the thought when a rocket exploded in the adjacent courtyard and knocked her flat on her face.

"I don't know what the hell to think!" David shouted back at her. "That last one was too close for comfort. If you haven't already done it, move into the corner of your cell. Get as much distance as possible between yourself and the outside wall, and keep your face covered. These guys don't have the greatest aim in the world."

Emma scrambled to her feet and dashed to the spot. The acrid stench of exploding bombs and the dense rain of mortar dust stung her eyes and filled her nose and lungs. Coughing, she wedged herself into the corner of her cell.

A sudden quiet settled over the cell block. Emma thought it as ominous as the sound of grenades and rockets exploding. "Now I know how those plastic ducks at the arcade feel."

David chuckled despite the chaos all around them, but Emma barely heard the sound. Instead she heard commands shouted in Arabic and rifle fire.

"I'm sorry I prayed for this, David. I really don't want us to die."

"We won't die, babe. With any kind of luck, this is our ticket out of the hotel from hell."

Blast after blast shook the cell block.

Emma clutched her cape, kept her head bowed, and remained crouched in the corner of her cell. During a ten-second respite she peered through a gap in the veil draped over her head. Disbelief flooded her when she spied a small hole in the wall of her cell.

"David! Can you hear me?"

Several successive explosions threw her across the floor, knocked the barred door of her cell askew, and increased the size of the hole in the rear cell wall. Emma gasped for air. Tendrils of flame danced along the overhead beams.

Emma gagged on the dense smoke that immediately filled her cell. Yet another explosion sent rubble tumbling across the floor. She felt a chunk of stone slam into her hip and couldn't smother a cry of pain.

Ceiling timbers cracked and splintered over-head, nearly drowning out David's voice as he yelled her name. A length of wood crashed to the floor, missing Emma's head by only a few inches. Heart racing, she bit back a scream and prayed for a reprieve.

More rubble tumbled across the backs of her legs. Still sprawled on the floor of her cell, she peered into the smoke and darkness, but couldn't see anything. Emma moaned, certain that she would die if she didn't find a way to escape her cell. But how? she wondered frantically as she dislodged chunks of stone and wood, struggled to her knees, and began to crawl across the floor. The deafening chaos of guerrilla warfare contin-ued to shriek in her ears.

"Emma, answer me, damn it!" David demanded.

A heartbeat later Emma felt strong hands seize her shoulders and yank her upright. Shocked, she cried his name and threw herself into his arms.

"This is our shot," he said urgently, his embrace fierce and protective. "We've got to make a run for it now."

She eased back, coughing because of the dense smoke. She could barely make out anything but the shape of his large frame as he towered over her. "Whatever we do, we do it together, David Winslow."

"That's my babe." He hugged her one last time, then grabbed her hand and cautioned, "Don't let go, no matter what happens."

Another rocket attack began, the assault on the prison growing more deadly by the second. David guided Emma from her cell through what had become a gaping hole in the seam of the cell's rear wall and the common wall that had separated them for the previous sixteen days. The ceiling caved in just seconds after they stepped into the courtyard.

Emma willingly followed David, instinctively trusting him to protect her from any and all threats.

They dodged armed soldiers shouting at one another in Arabic, ambulances speeding into the courtyard to collect the wounded, exploding mortar shells, and a seemingly endless series of screaming rockets that exploded all around them. Zigzagging through the sprawling prison compound, they soon located the front gate.

"It looks too easy," she whispered as they pressed their bodies into a darkened doorway and studied the open, unguarded prison entrance.

Emma glanced at David. She registered the shadows of fatigue under his hazel eyes, the tension tightening his strong jaw, the frown that marred his brow, and the smudges of dirt and mortar dust that covered him from head to toe. Not a pretty man by any means, but Emma nonetheless savored his raw masculinity and the security she felt just being at his side.

In turn David peered down at Emma. Pressed against the side of his body, clad in a shapeless native robe, and covered with grime and soot, she was still everything he'd imagined and much more. "We're going to have to chance it," he told her in a hoarse whisper. "Are you game?"

She nodded, ready to follow him into the fires of hell if he considered it necessary. Hadn't they already survived a version of hell?

A string of heavy tanks, followed by a half dozen jeeps and trucks, rolled through the open gates and roared past them. Hidden in the shadows of the doorway, Emma and David clung to each other, feeling each other's heartbeat and the tension stiffening their bodies.

Once again the area was deserted. David loosened his grip on Emma's waist and stared at her in silence. When he saw the glazed shock in her vivid blue eyes, he gently shook her and then gave her a moment to collect herself before saying, "I need to know the safest route to your friend's place."

She nodded and exhaled softly. "It's about three miles northeast of here. I visited her several times before . . . before . . ." She swallowed convulsively. "I've driven there at night, so it won't be hard to find."

He cupped her face with his big hands and tilted it upward. "We're going to make it, babe. Trust me."

Tears stung Emma's eyes and closed her throat, but she managed a nod and a shattered little smile that nearly drove David to his knees. He leaned down and tenderly pressed his lips to hers.

She clutched his waist, released a shaken sigh

that he greedily inhaled into his own lungs, and parted her lips to taste the sweetness within. When David eventually drew back, she whispered, "I trust you with my life and my heart."

Seven

Emma and David ran out of the prison compound and spent the next harrowing hours navigating the narrow alleyways and dark streets of the capital city in their attempt to escape notice. When they finally reached Mary Winthrop's house, they pounded on the front door. After receiving no answer, they walked around the house, tapping on every door and window. They returned to the front steps, and Emma cast a worried glance in David's direction. "It's obvious she's not home. What now?"

He exhaled wearily. "I'll have to jimmy the lock. We can't risk the noise of breaking a window."

"What about the Canadian embassy? It's not far from here."

He shook his head. When he spoke, his voice was lower and rougher than usual. "No time. It'll be light soon. We wouldn't make it."

"I'll keep watch," Emma whispered. She started

to slip away, but David snagged her wrist. She paused, aware that he sensed her growing panic.

"You're doing great, babe. I know you're dead on your feet, but I promise you I'll have us inside in no time."

She nodded, allowed herself a moment to absorb some of the strength reflected in his shadowed hazel eyes, and then sidled along the enclosed garden wall to the front gate. Residences loomed on either side of her.

Despite her concealing native garb, Emma feared being spotted and reported to government officials by an early-rising neighbor. And with the dawn poised to spill across the sky in a very short time, she knew they had to secret themselves within Mary Winthrop's two-bedroom home as soon as possible.

"Got it!" David announced a few minutes later.

Emma quickly retraced her footsteps, slipped inside the house ahead of David, and made it as far as the living room. Once there, she sank to her knees atop an ornate rug.

She yanked off the veil, tossed it aside, and wrapped her arms around herself to dispel the sudden chill she felt. David secured the front door, then made certain that all the windows in the house were covered.

Unable to stop herself, Emma began to tremble. Once David placed a lighted candle on a nearby coffee table, he dropped down beside her and gathered her into his arms. He held her as violent tremors rippled through her slender body.

After a time she regained her composure, but David continued to rock her as she leaned into the strength of his broad chest. Eventually she murmured, "Sorry."

"About what?" he asked as he rested his chin atop her bowed head.

"I think the last sixteen days just caught up with me." Embarrassed, she eased out of David's arms and climbed shakily to her feet.

He smiled tenderly and caught her hand before she turned away. "I was right about you, Emma Hamilton. You're impossibly beautiful."

She laughed, the sound nervous and filled with disbelief. Shoving her hair out of her face, she muttered, "I'm a disaster."

"A beautiful disaster," he clarified as he pulled himself to his feet, reclaimed the candle, and led her into the kitchen. They paused before a well-stocked pantry. "I'm starved. How about you?"

She risked a glance at him. She felt the searing, searching sweep of his dark eyes and immediately understood that he meant an altogether different kind of hunger. A tremor of expectation accelerated her heartbeat and made her breathless. Reaching up, she smoothed back the tumbled locks that had fallen across his forehead.

David captured her hand and pressed his mouth to her palm. He brushed his lips across the sensitive skin and sent a thousand fiery sensations cascading into her bloodstream. "I need to put my arms around you again," he confessed, moving nearer.

Emma held perfectly still, her eyes fastened to his rugged face. She trembled when he curved his free hand over her shoulder and tugged her forward. She desperately fitted her body to his and immediately felt his violent shudder, then the restraint he exercised over his powerful frame. The desire to be absorbed into his flesh and bones sang in her veins, but her underlying nervousness prevailed. She suddenly stiffened in his arms.

David exhaled regretfully, but freed her nonetheless. "Why don't you get cleaned up while I liberate some of the goodies in this pantry?"

Unable to meet his probing gaze, she stared at his chest. "You deserve to go first."

"You're tied up in knots, babe. A bath will help you relax."

She nervously smoothed her fingertips over the wrinkled robe she wore, nodded abruptly, and fled the room. As she drew a bath and shed her filthy clothing, Emma couldn't stop thinking about David's compassionate response to her erratic emotional state. She treasured his understanding, but she still felt foolish.

Emma settled into the tub. She attributed her case of nerves to the constant threat of discovery by the authorities, but her conscience contradicted her. Being alone with David had her thoroughly rattled, but why? she wondered in frustration.

How could she be nervous in the company of the man she loved and trusted? Even after she'd scrubbed her body, her long hair, and the clothes she'd worn, Emma still hadn't found an answer.

Clad in a thigh-length silk robe she'd borrowed from Mary's closet, she looked at herself in a mirror. So clean that her skin appeared flushed, and with her thick damp hair cascading across her shoulders and down her back, Emma saw that she looked younger and far more vulnerable than her twenty-six years.

David watched as she padded barefoot into the living room. He suddenly heaved himself to his feet and approached her. He froze, and something precious died a violent death within him when he saw her uneasy smile and the skittish sidestep she took.

"Relax and have something to eat," he suggested as he concealed his dismay. "I'll grab a shower, and then we can figure out our next move. No need to skimp on the food. There's plenty, and we can pay back your friend once we get home."

She nodded, her eyes huge and haunted before she looked away, leaned forward, and reached for a piece of cheese from the tray David had prepared. Before popping the morsel into her mouth, she said softly, "I filled the tub for you, and there are plenty of towels."

He closed his hands into fists to keep from reaching out for her. "We sound like polite strangers."

She sighed, her inability to meet his gaze telling him he was right on the money with that observation.

"How do you feel?" he asked, his eyes skimming

hotly over her silk-covered breasts, narrow waist, and shapely hips. Desire throbbed in his veins as he leisurely surveyed her long, slim legs, legs that seemed to go on forever, legs that made him want to moan aloud his desire to sheathe himself within her body and feel them wrapped around his hips in passion.

"I don't know how I feel. I guess I can't take it all in. A few hours ago, we . . . we were . . ." Her voice splintered.

He somehow managed to keep his hands off Emma, but the restraint demanded Herculean inner control. "We aren't going back to prison, so you can stop worrying as of right now."

"I'm afraid to believe we're on our way to freedom." She glanced up at him, then quickly looked away. "I can't help thinking about what they'll do to us if we're recaptured."

David thought about it constantly, but he refused to reveal his worry to Emma. "We aren't out of the woods yet, but we will be soon. You've been through a lot, babe. Why don't you—"

"Don't coddle me," she ordered sharply. "We both know you've been through far more, and you aren't falling apart over it."

His patience evaporated. "Then quit being so damn hard on yourself. I've been trained for this. You haven't. And for the record, you've been fantastic. I wouldn't have made it through the last sixteen days *and nights* if it hadn't been for you. Enough said?" he demanded.

Startled by his vehemence, she whispered,

"Enough said, David." She closed her eyes and massaged her forehead with her fingers. "I get a little crazy when I'm hungry and tired," she confessed. "I'll work this whole situation out in my head and then I'll be fine."

"Just hang on. There's no going back, so focus on the future and think positive thoughts."

When she opened her eyes, Emma discovered that David had disappeared down the dark hallway. She didn't really blame him for not wanting to deal with her at the moment. She felt very uncertain about the future.

Would they share the future, she wondered, or would he fade from her life once this crisis ended?

Idly picking at the food on the tray, she sorted through her confused emotions and finally accepted two indisputable facts. She was responding to the shock of being within touching distance of real freedom, and she feared that she would somehow fail David, especially if he had high expectations of her as a lover.

She eventually relaxed enough to remember that David Winslow wasn't the kind of man to criticize inexperience. Courageous, patient, and more sensitive to her feelings than any man she'd ever known, he'd been consistently compassionate and understanding of her. She had no reason to expect him to behave in any other way now that they were face-to-face.

She loved him, deeply, desperately, and completely. And although she doubted that he felt similarly, she wanted him with or without the safety net of a permanent commitment. Sighing softly, she silently vowed that she wouldn't let fear stand in her way where David was concerned.

The subject of her thoughts reappeared just as suddenly and as silently as he'd disappeared. Naked beneath the towel fastened low on his hips, he literally took Emma's breath away. Gone was the grime of deprivation and captivity. Gone were the tattered flight suit and heavy flight boots that he'd worn since being shot down. And gone was the thick beard that had obscured his hard cheeks and stubborn chin.

Scrubbed clean and freshly shaved, he looked like a new man. A strikingly attractive man, although not handsome in a conventional sense. He was big and powerful and so masculine that her heart raced as he moved into the living room with the lithe grace of a predator on the prowl.

He paused, a question in his eyes as he studied her with equal intensity. The strength of his character showed in his steely jaw, direct gaze, and sensual lips. His uncompromising personality seemed apparent in the rawboned sturdiness of a starkly male body marred by captivity but still vital enough to embrace tenderness or to endure harshness.

As they stared at each other, Emma wondered if David sensed the change, the profound rediscovery of self that had taken place within her during his absence. She exhaled shakily, thinking yet again that he was the embodiment of the classically rugged American male.

He made her ache with pure wanting, and she felt the heavy hotness of her blood as it flowed through her veins. She felt weakened and energized at the same time. She felt utterly seduced, and she felt incredibly needy, but only for his unique touch. He made her crave his caresses and induced a hunger within her soul that could only be sated by intimate knowledge of him.

Emma stared at David without pretense and without a shred of modesty. With her insides already heating like honey placed atop a flame, she grew feverish as she observed the subtle flex and flow of the muscles that crisscrossed his chest and flat belly when he breathed. She decided that she could watch him for the next hundred years.

Dark mahogany hair covered his chest and swirled downward in a sensual pattern that invited a fingertip inspection of the silky-looking pelt. *Her* fingertips, she decided. Only hers. She closed her hands into fists, but that only enflamed the desire that she knew was impossible to resist.

Getting to her feet, Emma shifted her eyes to David's chiseled features. He appeared to be cast in granite, but she knew that granite was cool to the touch and David wasn't. She'd felt his heat right down to her toes. He was a man composed of muscle and bone and sinew, a man of incredible warmth, a man who seduced as naturally as he breathed. He'd aroused her to the point of mindlessness with the simple stroking of his fingertips across the palm of her hand.

Silently shedding the nervousness and her anxiety that she might not please David, she then discarded her silk robe. She heard the hissing of his sudden inhalation and saw the tensing of his muscles and the rising evidence of his desire for her.

He remained still, but he watched her with a scorching gaze that nearly incinerated her soul. She moved toward him, pausing a few feet away. "I need to keep a promise."

"Promise?" he echoed blankly, mesmerized by her boldness. He explored every curve and hollow of her nakedness with hungry eyes. She was everything he'd imagined, everything he'd dreamed of possessing, everything he'd ever craved in a woman.

His desire for her engulfed him, making him tremble. His control started to disintegrate. Need thrummed inside him. He reached out, then withdrew his hand when his guilt assaulted him.

His conscience told him that he had no right to want Emma. She was too vulnerable and far too trusting where he was concerned, and she mattered too much for him to risk being careless or casual with her. And yet here she stood. Naked. Tantalizing. Enticing. His for the taking.

His gaze slowly drifted from the serenity reflected in her eyes and the gentle smile that graced her lips to the delicate curve of her shoulders and the unexpected bounty of her high, full breasts. They responded to his visual caress, swelling and firming beneath his gaze. Her nipples beaded, inviting his mouth. Tremors shook him, and yet he remained frozen in place.

His eyes shifted lower, taking in her tiny waist, the soft curve of her belly, the feminine width of her hips, and the thatch of black silk at the top of her thighs. Unable to stop himself, he groaned and reached out to her yet again.

This time he didn't withdraw his hands. This time he refused to resist the temptation to touch Emma, to hold her, to envision their bodies fitting together so completely that they ceased to be two separate beings.

As he cupped her breasts in his hands and brushed his thumbs back and forth across her taut nipples, he felt a succession of shudders rock her. He silently prayed that she wouldn't hate him later for taking advantage of her.

He also wondered which would be worse. Living with the knowledge that she'd made love with him because she knew he desired her and she was grateful enough for his support during their imprisonment. Or living with her resentment that he'd taken her at a weak moment, taken advantage of her in the way that no man had the right to take advantage of any woman, no matter how consuming his emotional need.

Emma closed the space that separated them. David inhaled sharply, the shock of her body heat, the softness of her skin, and the generous curves that shouted her femininity playing havoc with his sanity and his self-control. When she moaned low in her throat and burrowed against him, he held her as though she were the most precious thing in the world, his embrace both fierce and gentle.

"I wanted to hug you that first day," she murmured as she brushed her lips across the coarse hair covering his chest. "You were so patient with me." She peered up at him, her expression dreamy and her long hair a dense mane of damp black silk against the creamy beauty of her flawless skin.

"It wasn't long at all before I wanted to do more than simply put my arms around you. I found myself wanting us to share every intimacy possible between a man and a woman. I made other promises to myself as the days passed, David. Promises that I plan to keep now."

His heart thudded wildly in his chest, but he insisted, "You don't owe me anything."

"I owe you everything I have to give, but that's not really the point, is it?" she questioned as her fingers busied themselves with the knot that held his towel in place. She finally worked it free, tugged once, and revealed his arousal.

Emma experienced the heady satisfaction of knowing that David desired her as completely as she desired him. She teased the powerful hardness jutting from his body with the seductive swaying of her hips. Feeling the shudders that shook his body, she reveled in his response to her and in the strength of his embrace when he tightened his hold on her.

"What is the point?" he asked, his voice as rigid as the rest of him.

"I need you, and you need me." Lifting her arms, she laced her fingers together at the back of his neck and eased even closer. Her breasts plumped against his chest, her taut nipples branding him. "I want you, and you want me." She moaned at the sensations caused by their closeness. "I've dreamed about this for so long."

David buried his face in the curve of her neck. She shimmied against him, the delicate scrape of her nipples like tongues of fire against his skin. She shifted her hips once more, the erotic undulation of her lower body rousing David to unknown heights as he struggled to crush the reckless feelings storming through him.

Sensing his restraint and not understanding the reasons for it, Emma leaned back and peered questioningly up at him. He tightened his grip on her and kept their lower bodies joined even as they studied each other.

"Don't move." He sounded hoarse, and his expression reflected anguish. "Stay with me, babe. I need to hold you. I want to feel your heat and softness. I have to convince myself that you're real and not something I've imagined."

"I'm real." She settled more deeply into his embrace. "And you're incredibly real." She sighed tremulously. Her insides felt ripe and heavy and swollen, and she craved David with a depth of need that stunned her.

"Are you sure, babe?"

She nodded. "I want you, David, more than anyone or anything I've ever wanted in my entire life. You're the only person who can make me feel whole again."

He cupped the back of her head in his hands. Studying her upturned face, he marveled at the delicate beauty of her features, the vivid blue of her eyes, and the hunger reflected in her expression as she stared up at him.

"I ache for you, and I think I'll die if I don't have you, but I don't want to rush you, babe. You'd end up hating me, and I couldn't bear it if that happened."

She turned her head and pressed her lips into the palm of one of his hands, her tongue darting against his flesh. When she focused on his strained features a few moments later, she vowed, "I could never hate you."

"I want to believe you."

"Then believe me and love me, David Winslow, because *I'll* die if you don't. I need you to make the world disappear, if only for a few hours."

Honorable to the end, David insisted, "You might regret—"

She pressed her fingertips to his lips to silence him. "No matter what happens in the future, I will never regret anything we share."

The conviction in Emma's statement brought a swift conclusion to David's iron control. He succumbed to the sensual woman in his arms and to the molten desire streaming through his veins. Lowering his mouth to her lips, he kissed her until her knees threatened to buckle. He swung her up into his arms and carried her over to a grouping of overstuffed cushions in the living room.

Fingers laced together, they knelt face to face, chest to breasts, belly to belly, and thigh to thigh. Emma's lips whispered over the fading bruise that covered David's right shoulder, then worked their way across to his collarbone, the tip of her tongue leaving a hot trail of sensation in its wake. At the pulse point at the base of his throat, she pressed her lips against his flesh and absorbed the wild inner chanting of his body before she moved on to anoint his left shoulder.

With her fingertips she deftly skimmed the heated surface of his back before shifting her hands forward to his chest. She absorbed the strength of David's heartbeat and the heat of his skin when she tunneled her spread fingers into his thick chest hair. She closed her eyes, let her head fall back, and moaned softly while flexing her fingers against the strength and heat of his muscular upper torso.

David watched Emma through narrowed eyes, his maleness surging hungrily against the nest of silk at the base of her abdomen. He saw her find his nipples with ease, alternating back and forth between the two with catlike strokes of her tongue. Sensing her intent was to drive him insane with her sensual foray, he knew she was close to total success.

David seized her hands, raised them above her head, and then bent down to swirl his tongue across the tips of her breasts. Emma arched against him, trapping his manhood between her thighs.

He sipped and nipped and sucked at her raspberry-tinted nipples, bringing repeated gasps of pleasure and disbelieving cries to her lips. He simultaneously thrust against the damp, tender flesh at the apex of her thighs. She surged and bucked against him, torturing him in her quest to capture the long, hard ridge of flesh taunting her senses.

Releasing her hands, David tumbled her trembling body across the pillows and used his elbows to brace his upper body. She stilled when she saw the intense expression on his face. She held her breath as David nudged her thighs apart and probed the delicate folds of her body.

David claimed her lips and mouth. He proclaimed his possession of her with a tongue as adept as a skillfully wielded rapier. Repeatedly stabbing into the moist interior, he explored her at length, tasting her sweetness, stroking her depths, and then retreating to nibble at her full lower lip.

"Please," she whimpered brokenly.

He gazed at her, tension etched into his features while desire darkened his hazel eyes until they looked like bottomless black pools.

"David, please."

"Please what, babe?" He rotated his hips, taunting her lovingly, teasing her purposely, and drawing from her yet another moan of ecstasy.

Emma clutched his shoulders. "David . . . don't make me wait."

He eased back onto his haunches, drawing her

up and into his arms so that she was perched astride his thighs. He smiled and skimmed his fingertips along the inside of her upper thighs before tangling his fingers in the dark silk that concealed her feminine secrets.

When David quickly found the throbbing center of her sensuality, Emma's gasp of pleasure prompted him to intensify his stroking. He delved deeply into her heat with his fingers, feeling her searing wetness and the trembling of a hundred tiny muscles that promised the ultimate in pleasure.

He continued to stroke her until shivers rippled through her. Only then did he withdraw his fingers and urge her closer. He slid into her body without hesitation and welcomed the heated essence that consumed him.

He took her mouth a heartbeat later, inhaling her breathless and ecstatic cries. He immediately felt the possessive clutch of her body right down to his toes.

Wrapping her arms around his neck, Emma circled his narrow hips with her long, slim legs. David felt like a captive, but this time he was a willing prisoner of the heart. Clasping her buttocks, he repeatedly surged into her depths as she clung to him.

Urgency drove them to a frantic pace, and they burned for each other in a conflagration so complete, they lost touch with everything but the currents of pleasure arcing between their bodies.

Emma suddenly came apart in David's hands.

He heard her gasp in disbelief, and she repeated his name over and over again as her body stiffened. The shocking wildness of her climax when it claimed her ravaged his control and forced him to surrender to his own impending release. David thrust high and hard, again and again until he exploded within the scalding heat of Emma's body.

Afterward he cradled her against his chest and lowered their joined bodies to the cushions. Still shaken, he couldn't find the words to express the emotions she evoked, so he simply savored the closeness they'd shared and held her to his heart.

Emma sighed, her breath warm against David's throat as she tucked her head beneath his chin, curled into his warmth, and whispered, "I love you."

After drawing a cotton throw over their bodies, he tightened his embrace but said nothing in response to her declaration of love. Her breathing eventually slowed, and she fell into a deep sleep.

Still convinced that Emma's feelings for him had been shaped by the circumstances of their imprisonment, David felt reluctant to reveal the true extent of his own emotions. That he loved Emma wasn't the point. Neither one of them could predict how she would feel once they were free and he was no longer the center of her world. That, unfortunately, *was* the point.

David held Emma for several hours, watching over her while she slept. Although exhausted himself, he knew better than to let down his guard as long as they remained in the capital city. He silently prayed that he would be able to get Emma to the Canadian embassy before the day ended. Above all else he wanted her safe, even if it meant risking his life or losing her love.

Eight

Sprawled on her back, Emma stretched content-edly. Lips she immediately recognized whispered up the side of her neck and paused at a particu-larly sensitive spot just below her ear.

David nibbled at her tender skin, sending chill bumps all the way down to her toes. Emma made a faint purring sound before she opened her eyes to find him beside her, his upper body propped on an elbow.

"What a lovely way to wake up," she murmured.

Turning onto her side, Emma rolled toward him. She brought her hand up to his cheek, then lightly trailed her fingernails down the side of his beard-stubbled face. All the while she basked in the sturdiness of his large-framed body and in the warmth reflected in his steady gaze.

"I was afraid I'd dreamed this morning," she admitted softly.

David smiled and stroked the graceful curve of

her hip with his free hand. "You're well on your way to convincing me that dreams periodically come true."

"Mine certainly did."

Emma leaned forward, slid her hand across his shoulder to the back of his neck, and pressed her lips to the pulse point at the base of his throat. Her nipples tingled as they brushed against his chest hair. Deep inside she felt tiny flames ignite. She shivered helplessly, once again at the mercy of the emotions and desires David evoked in her heart and body.

Sighing, she lifted her head and peered up at him. His hand stilled on her hip. Emma watched his smile fade and his eyes darken as she eased her lower body into more intimate contact with his loins. She immediately felt the strength of his body's response to her closeness.

"You want me again," she breathed with delight.

David gave her a look that made her think of a wolf closing in on his prey. "I'll always want you, babe." His hand drifted to the small of her back. He pressed her more snugly to the hard ridge of flesh throbbing against her abdomen.

Emma felt streamers of sensations unfurl in her veins. She caught her breath when David gathered her close, rolled onto his back, and drew her atop his powerful body. She held very still as he brought his hands up to frame her face, and she silently savored his possessiveness when he plunged his fingers into the disheveled mane that cascaded around them like a dark veil.

"Does it surprise you that I want you again?"

She shook her head. "I want you too."

"You're as soft and as sensual as I knew you'd be."

Emma flushed, glad that he thought of her that way. "I worried that you might be disappointed."

"You couldn't disappoint me. Not in a million years." David closed his eyes as tension suddenly infused his body.

Emma assumed that he was simply reacting to their intimate alignment, especially when the fingers massaging her scalp flexed and then tightened. She idly traced his dark brows with her fingertips, then trailed them past his temples to his cheeks.

"I wouldn't have made it without you these last few weeks, babe. The isolation was destroying my sanity."

The rawness of his voice and the sudden shift in his mood startled Emma. Her fingers stilled, and she studied him closely. The grimace marring his rugged features, and the trembling now consuming his entire body made her guess that he was grappling with some particularly hellish memories.

"You gave me hope and a reason to fight back," he continued. "I'll always be grateful to you for what you've done."

"We helped each other," Emma reminded him softly. She didn't want his gratitude, but she suddenly feared that she wanted the impossible from David. Love, she knew, had to be given as a gift. It couldn't be forced.

David's fingers clenched yet again as he gripped her head. Emma felt the tension coursing through him. She sensed that he'd suppressed his own anxiety to help her through the last few weeks, and she finally grasped the full extent of his vulnerability.

Emma smoothed her fingertips along the side of his face in an effort to calm him. She felt his hold ease, but she still worried over the anguish in the depths of his hazel eyes and the edge in his low voice, grittier than usual, when he finally spoke.

"I need you to love me, babe. I can't stop thinking about the last two and a half months. My mind won't let me shut it off." He blinked and finally focused on her face. "Love me, please. Help me forget for just a little while."

Swallowing the tears threatening to choke her, Emma slowly leaned forward. David's hands dropped away from her head, and she felt them glide unsteadily over her shoulders and down her back before pausing at her hips. Though she'd never loved anyone as much as she loved him at this moment, it suddenly didn't matter that he might not love her back.

She pressed her lips to his. Slowly and very tenderly, she ran the tip of her tongue across his lower lip. David trembled beneath her caress, and a new kind of tension began to seep into his body. Smoothing his hands back and forth across Emma's hips, he ignited sensations all over her sensitive skin with his callused fingertips.

She nipped at his lower lip before venturing

beyond to sample his heat. Capturing his tongue with gentle teeth, she silently vowed that she would use her feelings for him as a healing balm.

Love and desire mingled within her as she savored David's unique taste and explored the varying textures of his mouth. When she sucked at his tongue, David responded by dipping his fingers between her parted thighs. She moaned, drew in a strangled breath, and intensified their kiss when she felt his questing fingers delve deeply into the wet heat awaiting him.

She'd been hurled into the center of a raging storm. Breathless and thoroughly aroused, she shifted restlessly atop David. She hungrily devoured his mouth as she clung to him. Her breasts aching for the feel of his hands, she grew almost frantic as her nipples turned to taut points of blistering desire.

She eventually relinquished his lips and moved like hot satin down his muscular torso. She teased and tantalized and dazzled him with hot kisses and the provocative stroking of her fingertips.

Inexperience made her pause briefly at his hips, but then Emma found the courage she needed to express her love for David.

She felt his shock and heard his muted cry of disbelief as she closed her mouth around him. Emboldened by his response, she devoted herself to transporting David far beyond the anguish of his recent memories. She reduced his world to blurred sensations, tingling nerve endings, and sensual cravings. And just as she'd given him the gift of her love, she gave of herself, without restraint, without concern for her own needs, and without conditions.

Emma eventually drew back and retraced the route of her consuming caresses as she moved back up David's shaking body. She made the journey at a leisurely pace, lingering to press a gentle kiss to a fading bruise along the edge of his ribs, pausing to drag the tip of her tongue over a flat male nipple.

She shifted atop him once more, her hips poised above his pulsing shaft, her breasts plumped against his broad chest. About to lower her lips to his, she gasped when he closed his hands around her waist and moved her all the way forward until she straddled his shoulders.

As he clasped her parted thighs, her startled gaze dropped down to his face, but the fire burning in his eyes froze her in place and kept her from protesting.

She trembled as he smoothed his fingertips up the silken skin of her inner thighs, his intent clear when he glanced at her and then very deliberately stroked her most sensitive flesh. Emma's eyes fluttered closed. She moaned.

Gently insistent masculine hands urged her even closer. Emma didn't resist. Tremors of sweet sensation swept up her thighs and into her abdomen, and her body clenched and unclenched. She felt a new kind of hunger invade her.

"David?"

"Trust me, babe," he whispered urgently.

"I do."

He brought his lips to her feminine secrets, tenderly returning the intimate kisses she'd bestowed upon him only minutes earlier.

Emma knew she would eventually die of the pleasure, but she no longer cared. She felt her senses expand with each erotic and exotic caress. When he closed his mouth over her, aggressive yet also gloriously tender, she groaned aloud. He became the center of her universe, and he thrilled her with a diligent tongue that rasped over responsive flesh and hands that stroked and massaged her thighs and hips.

None of Emma's fantasies had prepared her for David's sensual assault. He skimmed his fingertips up her body and closed her hands over her breasts, then simultaneously sipped at her and plucked her nipples to tight pebbles of desire with his fingertips.

She swayed suddenly, the air shuddering in and out of her lungs as she struggled to remain balanced above him. David guided her down to the cushions, tucking her beneath him, kneeling between her parted thighs.

He paused then, his smoldering gaze sweeping over her face and breasts. Quivering with need, Emma wondered if that was love shining in David's eyes.

Determined to have his strength within her, she clasped his hips and discovered that he needed little urging. She buried her face in the curve of his shoulder, a scream of relief lodged in her throat as he thrust into her body.

Slipping his arms around her, he brought her up against his broad chest and surged even more deeply into her. Emma's breath caught and then was released in a rush of pleasure. She sensed that in burying himself in the grasp of her body, David was relinquishing the desperate emotions of the preceding months in favor of a sensory journey of healing love.

Their pace soon matched the frantic cadence of their racing hearts. Emma splintered and then spasmed. She came apart within in the safe harbor of David's arms, clinging to him, too breathless to speak.

Shocked and awed by what they'd shared, they held each other tightly as startling aftershocks tremored through their bodies. It took time, but their breathing eventually slowed to normal.

Emma stilled David a short while later when he began to shift away from her. "Stay with me."

He snugged her against his sweat-drenched body and rolled them to their sides. "I don't want to crush you."

She smiled at his concern, her lips curving against his throat.

When he peered down at her, she felt a renewed sense of peace flowing through him. "You're amazing, babe."

She pressed her cheek to his chest, needing to hold reality at bay for just a little while longer. "Nothing like that's ever happened to me before. It was everything you said it would be, and then even more."

He eased backward a few inches and tipped her chin up with his fingertips so that he could see her face. "I've never known anyone like you."

"That makes us even."

"It makes us lucky."

She smiled again, still shaken inside, and her eyes sparkled with unshed tears. "More than lucky."

"Much more," he agreed. Lifting her hand, he brought it to his lips, pressed his mouth to her palm, and touched the center with the tip of his tongue.

Emma breathed shakily. Even his most playful touch aroused her. Curving her hand over his cheek, she said, "Why don't you rest for a while? It's my turn to watch over you while you sleep."

He grinned. "Equality of the sexes and all that stuff, huh?"

She could see the exhaustion in his features, so she tugged his face closer and planted a quick little kiss on his lips before she pulled herself up to sit at his side. "Turnabout's fair play, so no arguments."

He gave her a casual salute before rolling onto his back. "Thanks, babe." David slanted a glance in her direction, obviously wanting to say something but not sure how to manage it. "For everything," he said awkwardly.

Emma glanced away before she could tell him how deeply and desperately she loved him. She knew this wasn't the time, but she wondered if there would ever be a right time. She rubbed her forehead with her fingertips, uncertainty gnawing at her and eroding a small portion of the joy she'd found in David's arms.

He reached out and ran his fingers up and down her back. "Why so pensive all of a sudden?"

Forcing herself to smile, she managed a bright-eyed look. "Just planning my wardrobe for tonight's expedition."

He frowned, and Emma realized he was too familiar with her to accept such a superficial explanation. "You aren't telling me the truth. Why?"

"I'm nervous about tonight, that's all." She hadn't lied, she told herself. She simply hadn't told him the entire truth, which made it even more difficult for her to keep meeting his gaze.

His expression gentled. "We'll make it."

She caught his hand after he trailed his fingers over her shoulder and down the high slope of her breast. After lacing their fingers together, she nodded and then pressed her lips to the back of David's hand.

Emma tugged the burka she'd found in Mary's bureau over her head and adjusted the headpiece so that only her eyes were visible. She looked at it critically and was pleased that it fit so well.

Once she added the veil and black robe to her costume, she hoped she'd look like any other Arab woman making her way through the streets of the capital city, in spite of her bright blue eyes. "So I'll squint a lot," she muttered. Should they be stopped, explaining to the authorities why she was out past curfew would be the real challenge, she realized.

"We'll just have to be extra careful," she reminded herself.

Emma removed the burka, tucked it and her heavy veil into the pocket of her jeans, and put on the still-damp robe she'd laundered earlier in the day.

David walked into the bedroom and paused behind Emma. She studied his reflection in the mirror with the help of the flickering light from a candle placed nearby. Tall, rugged, and too sexy for words, he wore a makeshift attire that made him resemble a roguish-looking Middle East sheik. The fact that his hair had grown long enough during captivity to curl at his neck and tumble haphazardly across his forehead helped too. A traditional Marine Corps haircut would have signaled David's identity to the locals in short order.

Turning to face him, she carefully inspected the length of yard goods she'd arranged on him and pinned into place to conceal his flight suit and boots. Since Mary Winthrop was single and didn't have any masculine native clothing in her closet, they'd been forced to improvise with a bolt of fabric they'd found in her sewing room.

"You'll have to be careful when you walk," she noted as she circled around him. "All those zippered pockets on the arms and legs of your flight suit might show." She frowned. "I just wish I'd been able to fashion a burnoose for you."

David curved his hands over her shoulders and drew her against his body. "Relax. It's nearly midnight. No one's going to be checking out my wardrobe."

She exhaled, the sound an echo of the apprehension she felt. "Sorry. I'm just nervous. We were lucky last night."

"Our luck will hold. All the usual chaos is going on outside. You know as well as I do that it starts up just after dark every single night, and it doesn't ease until dawn. These people are too busy trying to bomb each other into the Stone Age to pay much attention to us. Our real challenge is not getting caught in the cross fire."

She forced herself to step back, square her shoulders, and smile up at him, in spite of the fact that she wanted to find a cave on the other side of the planet and hide there in the safety of his arms until the world became a more peaceful place. "I'll be all right once we're on our way. Waiting is the difficult part."

David winked at her. "We'll blow this popsicle stand in a few minutes. Did you leave a note for your friend, just in case she's not at the embassy when we get there?"

Emma nodded. "I tucked it into the cookie jar." She grinned when she saw his disbelief, and some of her tension left her. "Trust me. That's how we left messages for each other when we were in college."

He cupped her face with his hand, the tenderness in his eyes making her heart flutter. "I trust you, babe. You're the only person I do trust."

In spite of her promise to herself to remain strong, she asked, "We're going to make it, aren't we, David?"

"Or die trying," he ground out harshly.

Emma flinched. David didn't seem to want to acknowledge her reaction. He simply slipped his arm around her shoulder, collected the candle she'd used while dressing, and nudged her in the direction of the front room.

Unwilling to avoid the truth any longer, Emma eased free of David when they reached the living room. "Whatever happens to us tonight, I want you to know that the last seventeen days with you have been the best days of my life."

He stepped forward, but hesitated when she insisted, "Please, let me finish. I really need to say this before we leave."

His expression unreadable, David nodded and remained motionless less than two feet from Emma.

"You're my most treasured friend and my lover. Your strength and courage and the knowledge you've willingly shared have helped me keep my hopes alive. You've also been more tender with me and more sensitive to my needs than the man I once thought I loved." Unable to look at him until now, she lifted her gaze and whispered the feelings etched into her soul. "I love you, David Winslow. I will always love you."

He moved forward, grabbed her, and yanked her against his chest, his usual gentleness gone. "I love you, too, babe," he declared.

He kissed her then, a kiss so powerful that

Emma felt the impact in the depths of her heart. When David finally released her, she realized that, whatever happened in the hours ahead, she was more alive than ever before.

"Let's go home, babe."

Smiling through the tears filling her eyes, Emma nodded. Hand in hand, they faced the unknown once again as they departed Mary Winthrop's home and slipped silently into the chaotic night.

Nine

Despite the relentlessly screaming air-raid sirens, the weeping women and terrified children seeking shelter from exploding bombs, and men armed with portable rocket launchers on every other street corner, Emma and David managed to blend in.

David kept a tight grip on Emma's hand as they dodged roving bands of guerrillas. He feared that a grenade or a rocket explosion might kill them, but he knew they had no choice but to risk seeking refuge at the Canadian embassy. They periodically hid in abandoned buildings, holding each other in the darkness as they waited for lulls in the street fighting.

Shortly after midnight Emma and David arrived at the front gates of the Canadian embassy. Greeted with understandable suspicion by the guards at the compound, David insistently and repeatedly identified himself as an American military officer. He refused to be turned away. Emma's panic increased when her claim that she was a friend of an embassy employee was ignored.

David finally persuaded the uniformed men to summon the duty security officer, a balding, middle-aged fellow with a British accent, who quickly hustled them into the embassy.

"Even though you're both down a few pounds, I recognize you from the photos your State Department people forwarded to us," Mr. Winston remarked with a casualness that implied missing Americans showed up on his doorstep regularly.

"Missing, but not forgotten," David said with some satisfaction. He kept Emma in the circle of his arm as they crossed the deserted foyer.

Winston nodded, his expression sober. "We've had heavy message traffic on you both," he told them as he led the way to an upstairs suite. Throwing open the double doors, he stepped aside and waved them inside. "Make yourselves comfortable while I summon the ambassador. He won't believe you're both alive until he sees you for himself."

Shedding his disguise on a nearby chair, David felt relieved to have Emma inside the relative safety of the embassy. The relationship between the United States and Canada, he knew, was a strong one, and numerous Americans trapped in the Middle East during times of conflict had survived due to Canadian generosity and cleverness.

David kept a close watch on Emma, his worry over her state of mind momentarily displacing his concerns about how they would exit the country without detection by government authorities.

Drained by the latest leg of their journey to freedom, Emma jerked off her costume, adding it to the pile David had started. She sidestepped him when he reached out to her, barely registering the distress that flared in his eyes at being rebuffed.

Wandering aimlessly around the spacious sitting room, she paused briefly to slide her fingertips across the surface of an oak library table. Emma sighed audibly before moving on to examine a bouquet of fresh flowers on a coffee table that separated two gray linen-covered couches.

To David she appeared dangerously pale and fragile. Her silence distressed him, and her expression, as well as her trembling, hinted that she was remembering the violence they'd witnessed in the streets.

He doubted that either of them would ever forget what they'd seen or endured, but he reminded himself that as time passed, their memories would fade. He prayed he was right, especially where Emma was concerned.

As he studied her, he absently noted that the weight she'd lost in recent weeks emphasized her slim-limbed frame, the delicacy of her bone structure, and the smudged shadows of fatigue and lingering fear beneath her eyes. He allowed himself the luxury of visually skimming the flaring width of her hips, her minuscule waist, and the generous shape of her breasts.

He knew this woman intimately, and yet he experienced a sudden yearning within his heart to know her with even greater intimacy. He wanted the knowledge of her first thoughts each morning and her final thoughts each night before she drifted off to sleep in his arms. He also wanted time to learn all the facets of her personality—what made her cry, what she considered tedious, and what made her happy. He wanted to see once again the sensual smile he'd glimpsed when they'd made love, and he craved the healing passion of her embrace and the earth-shattering pleasure of sinking into the moist depths of her body. Most of all, he wanted their love to last ten lifetimes.

David felt his body's reaction to his fantasies, and he consciously put the brakes on his rising need. Approaching Emma, he stopped her restless pacing by stepping into her path and forcing her to acknowledge his presence. "Relax, babe. We're halfway home."

She stared up at him, her face pale, her blue eyes dazed-looking. Holding on to his outstretched arms, she dug her fingers into his biceps as she clutched at him, and her voice quivered as she spoke. "Will they really be able to get us out of here?"

David quickly gathered her against his body. "If they can't, we'll find another way out."

She turned her face into the curve that joined his broad shoulder and strong neck, while her arms snaked around his waist. "I feel like I'm on the verge of screaming my lungs out, and I can't seem to stop shaking."

"You've held in your fear too long, babe. It was bound to come out eventually. You're just reacting to what we've been through tonight. We'll survive this together, so scream or cry or kick something. Do whatever you need to do, because when you're finished, I'll still be here waiting for you. I'm not going anywhere without you."

Tears filled her eyes and fell like hot summer rain, wetting his neck and shoulder as he held her and comforted her with all the tenderness and love he felt for her.

David heard footsteps, but didn't release Emma. He saw the security officer step into the open doorway and felt immensely grateful for the compassion in the man's face.

"You're in luck," he told them quietly. "We've got a supply plane coming in first thing in the morning. My people are working out a way to get you two on it without anyone being the wiser." He hurried off once David nodded in response to his news.

Alone again, David guided Emma to one of the couches. He tugged her down beside him and hugged her against the hard wall of his chest.

"I will never get used to the violence people are capable of inflicting on each other," she admitted as she wiped away her tears. "Did you see all those poor children? I'll never forget the terror in their little faces. Never," she whispered brokenly.

Her voice increased the ache in his heart. He rested his chin atop her head, gently running his hands up and down her arms and back in an effort to soothe her. Sensing she had more to say, he remained quiet.

"I'm shocked we made it this far."

He brought her even more snugly against his body. His own anxiety had nearly eaten him alive during the previous twenty-four hours. Like Emma, he was amazed that their luck hadn't run out yet.

As for the violence they'd witnessed and the cruelty they'd endured, the warrior in him couldn't muster any surprise. Good and evil existed, he realized with a heavy sigh, and episodes of inhumanity occurred in the world.

"David?"

He glanced down at her upturned face. Wide-eyed and still dangerously pale, she stared at him. He ignored the faint warning of his conscience, lowered his head, and pressed his lips to hers. His love for her burst from him with lightning speed as he plunged his tongue into the depths of her mouth.

Emma arched into him, hungry for his kiss as she responded to him with equally intense passion. With a throaty moan she abandoned herself to his seductive assault even as she derived comfort within his fierce embrace. A rough brand of sensuality tinged their appetites for each other, making them breathless, reducing them to quivering nerve endings and the most basic instincts.

Several minutes passed before they heard a polite cough. Protected from view by David's large frame, Emma shuddered and sagged against him. He held her, allowing them both time to pull themselves together before they faced their unexpected audience.

They reluctantly eased apart. Emma gave David a damp but wry smile. Chagrined, he felt like an adolescent as he got to his feet. But despite the anguished desire flaring in his loins, David was still beyond being embarrassed. At the moment he cared little about what anyone thought of him. His only concern was getting Emma out of the Middle East.

"Major Winslow, Miss Hamilton, welcome to Canadian soil, despite the limited borders of this particular piece of real estate. I'm Ambassador Highgate," he said, shaking hands with David. "You'll be safe here. I must say, it's a relief to see that you're both alive and in fairly good health. We only recently learned that you were being held in the same prison and in the same cell block."

"You have excellent informants, Mr. Ambassador." David sat back down beside a subdued Emma. Reclaiming her hand, he discovered that she'd stopped shaking. "We appreciate your hospitality, sir."

He waited for the ambassador, a gray-haired gentleman clad in silk pajamas, smoking jacket, and leather slippers, to make himself comfortable on the opposite couch before prompting, "Your security officer mentioned message traffic."

The ambassador nodded. "All very secure, I assure you. Once we confirmed that you and Miss Hamilton were still alive, we immediately notified your State Department. We've been in constant touch with them for the last few weeks."

The older man leaned forward and tapped the contents of his pipe into a crystal ashtray. "We knew, of course, about your last mission, Major. The American, Canadian, and European media people haven't let the story die, especially since reconnaissance missions were, and still are, legitimate features of the cease-fire agreement, but it wasn't until Miss Hamilton was placed in your cell block that one of our more reliable information sources identified your precise location and reported back to us."

"We weren't certain that anyone even knew where we were," Emma remarked.

He smiled at her. "Certain diplomatic sources, which will have to remain unnamed to ensure their safety, assured us that Major Winslow was still alive, although we were routinely denied an opportunity to see him on behalf of our American colleagues. We conveyed what little we knew to the appropriate officials in Washington on a regular basis, but our inability to verify your physical well-being, Major, left us at a distinct disadvantage."

"They could've killed me right away," David said bluntly. "Fortunately they considered me an interesting diversion and kept me around for their amusement."

The ambassador clearly understood David's meaning, but he tactfully turned his attention back to Emma. "And you, Miss Hamilton. You were missed almost immediately. First by our Miss Winthrop, who said you didn't attend a dinner engagement, and then by the Child Feed authorities in Europe and in America. It took us a few days and several bribes, but we finally established that you'd been detained by the secret police for lack of proper travel documents. Unfortunately we were also denied an opportunity to check on you."

"You obviously tried, Ambassador Highgate, so please don't apologize. It's a relief to know that someone was looking out for us, especially since we don't have an embassy here at present."

"You must be exhausted, my dear."

"We both are," she admitted. "Would it be possible for me to speak with Mary?"

"Miss Winthrop's absent at present. She took family leave to be with her father."

Emma straightened in alarm. "Not another heart attack?"

The ambassador didn't try to conceal his surprise. "You do know our Mary and her family quite well, don't you?"

Emma nodded. "We've been friends since college."

"Mary's father is getting a pacemaker. Tomorrow, I believe. It seems he's finally strong enough to undergo the surgery."

"David and I hid in her house today. I left her a note. She'll know where to look for it when she returns."

The ambassador got up from the couch and walked around the long, low coffee table separating him from David and Emma. They both stood too.

"Since the prison authorities rarely release their prisoners willingly, I have to assume you engineered your own escape. Care to tell me how you managed it, or would you prefer to wait for debriefing by your own people?"

David smiled the satisfied smile of a man who'd survived in spite of staggering odds. "It was nothing more than an accident of fate, sir. Someone blew out the wall in our cell block about twenty-four hours ago. We've been on the run ever since."

Ambassador Highgate shook his head in wonder. David concluded by his expression that, had they been caught, they would have faced a firing squad.

"Amazing! As I indicated, we've attempted to gain access to you both via diplomatic channels. Storming the prison wasn't an option, I'm afraid, although there was some indication—rather an oblique indication, I might add—that one of your covert military teams was preparing to try to extract you, Major."

David nodded. He'd prayed that such an attempt would be made on his behalf. Despite the lack of success, he appreciated the fact that he hadn't been abandoned or forgotten.

"What about our families?" Emma asked. "Can we let them know we're all right?"

"I'm afraid not, at least not right now. There's always the risk that information about you could leak, no matter how secure our communications system might be. If that were to happen, then you'd compromise my staff and you could easily find yourselves residents of the embassy. Until cooler heads prevail in the government and the dictator is ousted, I'm afraid a siege mentality prevails in this country. It wouldn't do for you to be trapped here indefinitely."

David squeezed Emma's hand and glanced down at her. "Patience, babe."

She smiled for the first time that night, aware that her eagerness to be free had momentarily gotten in the way of more practical matters.

"Your State Department and military will handle notification of your families," the ambassador continued. "My people will focus on getting you two out of the country at the earliest possible moment, which will probably be tomorrow morning, if Mr. Winston, our security officer, has his way. He was once with British Intelligence, so you can probably imagine some of the clandestine tricks he's got up his sleeve for occasions such as this one."

Emma smothered a yawn as she leaned against David. The ambassador appeared sympathetic to her obvious fatigue.

"Why don't you get some rest, Miss Hamilton? One of my aides will arrive shortly with refreshments for you, as I'm certain your meals haven't been of a sumptuous nature in recent weeks." Gesturing with a free hand, he explained, "This is the sitting room for a two-bedroom suite. Each bedroom has a private bath. If you need medical attention, we have a nurse on staff, and your laundry can be seen to while you rest."

"Thank you, Ambassador Highgate, for everything." Emma stepped forward. "All I really need is a long soak in a hot tub and some sleep. I'm afraid the stress of dodging bullets has worn me out."

"Certainly, my dear." He took her extended hand, his manner reflecting the courtliness of a bygone era, and patted it kindly. "You've obviously been very courageous throughout your ordeal. If you were my daughter, I know I'd be enormously proud of you."

She flushed, thinking that any courage she possessed had come from David. She glanced at the man who dominated both her heart and her thoughts.

The ambassador turned to David. "Major, I'll need to speak with you privately before you retire. Your State Department will require certain information, as I'm certain you already realize. After that, your time is your own until Mr. Winston is ready for you."

"Certainly, sir." David hugged Emma and promised softly, "I'll be in soon."

She nodded, flashed a parting smile at the ambassador, and went to the bedroom. She closed the door behind her and sank back against it. Looking around the finely appointed room, she couldn't help comparing it with the filthy cell she'd recently occupied. Emma shivered, cast aside the memory, and headed for the bathroom.

David found Emma in bed after he finished his conversation with the ambassador and the embassy security officer. He stood at the end of the bed, his heart bumping erratically in his chest as he studied her in repose. Naked beneath a thick, ankle-length terry robe that was belted at the waist, she lay sprawled on her back, her long black hair like a length of black satin as it framed her face and tumbled across her pillow.

Leaning down, David ran his fingertips up the length of her exposed leg before pressing a light kiss to her forehead. Although she moaned and whispered his name, he forced himself to back away from her.

David knew she needed to sleep, almost as much as he needed to feel her avid mouth and tender touch skimming down his body, lingering here to tantalize, pausing there to torment. Shaken by his hunger for Emma, David abruptly turned away from her and strode into the bathroom.

Stripping to the skin, he stepped under the needle-sharp spray of a hot shower. He stood there until the muscles in his body began to relax and the hunger he felt for Emma receded. And he repeatedly reminded himself that he owed them both time to think, time to be certain that being together once they returned to their respective lives was what they both really wanted.

After placing their soiled clothes outside the bedroom door, David extinguished the bedside lamp she'd left on for him and joined her. Drawing Emma close, he pulled a quilt over their bodies.

David held her, absently noting the sound of an

air-raid siren in the distance and trying not to think of the next leg of their journey to freedom that would ultimately end with their parting.

Emma jerked awake at the sound of someone knocking on the bedroom door. David's arm, resting across her midriff, instantly tightened. A moment later, he lifted his tousled head and peered sleepily at Emma.

"Someone's at the door," she whispered.

He grunted and forced himself out of bed. Snagging the towel he'd abandoned before crawling into bed, he secured it at his hips and yanked open the door. Emma tugged the covers to her chin and listened.

"You've got forty-five minutes to dress and eat," Winston told David. "Canadian passports and assorted travel documents required to depart the country have been prepared for you."

"Then we're leaving in the open?" he asked, taking the papers and clean clothes Winston held out to him.

Winston nodded. "The less subterfuge, the better. The airport guards are less likely to challenge you that way. Any problems?"

"None. We'll be ready."

Emma watched the two men shake hands. She wondered if they would see Mr. Winston again, but she doubted it, because she sensed that he was a man who preferred to remain in the background.

David closed the door and turned to face Emma, who'd drawn herself up against the headboard. The lapels of her robe gaped open, and he caught a tantalizing glimpse of cleavage that almost made him groan aloud.

He forced himself to study their phony passports. "Feel like pretending to be Charlotte Truesdale from Toronto today?"

"I'll pretend to be a rabbit who pops out of a magician's hat if it'll get me home," she declared as she flipped back the covers and scooted across the bed.

Moving quickly, she exposed the long, shapely legs David immediately coveted around his hips. With tremendous effort he redirected his gaze to the passports as Emma strolled into the bathroom.

They said little as they hurriedly dressed. For David the resourceful Mr. Winston had secured a long raincoat, an ill-fitting pair of slacks, pullover sweater, and deck shoes, along with a small duffel bag for his flight suit and boots. Then they stepped into the sitting room, where they found breakfast awaiting them. Although Emma barely tasted her food, she managed to drink a glass of orange juice and eat a small bowl of hot cereal.

David, she noticed, ate like a man consuming his last meal. She didn't voice her observation, sensing that it would take a while before he believed that he would eat regularly again. One of the hazards, she decided, of being incarcerated and not knowing if you'd ever be free once more.

They departed the Canadian embassy in a limo and with an openness that declared they were simply visiting members of the diplomat corps with nothing whatever to hide. The driver and the man riding shotgun focused on the crowded roadway and didn't initiate conversation. On the advice of the ambassador, who wished them a safe trip home and accepted a hug of thanks from Emma, they tried to appear relaxed.

Forty-five minutes later Emma barely contained her shock and delight that they'd outwitted the airport security guards and customs personnel with such incredible ease. Sinking into one of the lumpy seats that lined one side of the aircraft's cargo hold, she buckled her seatbelt and stared straight ahead.

David joined her a few minutes later, dressed in his own clothes, and quickly secured his seatbelt. She felt him settle back in his seat as the aircraft began to lumber down the runway. Glancing at him, she noticed the grim expression on his face. A tremor of surprise rippled through her.

When David didn't look at or speak to her during the hour-and-a-half flight to Damascus, Emma tried to tell herself it was because of the excessive noise the cargo plane made. When she attempted to lace their fingers together after they were transferred to an American military aircraft on the Damascus runway, he shook his head without even glancing at her and moved to the cockpit to chat with the flight crew.

Hurt and bewildered, Emma didn't understand

David's withdrawal from her, which only intensified as they flew the five hours to Germany. Polite,
but still silent and restrained, he then helped her
into a helicopter for the fifteen-minute ride from
Rhein Main Air Force Base to the American Hospital at Wiesbaden, the destination of almost all
American citizens held against their will in the
Middle East.

She stared at him when he turned to her once the
helicopter touched down. "Take care, babe. I'll . . .
I'll see you," he said, his hungry gaze sweeping over
her face as though to memorize each and every
feature.

Too stunned to move, Emma watched David exit
the aircraft, salute the American flag rippling in
the breeze on a nearby flagpole, and then greet the
Marine Corps officers waiting for him at the edge
of the helipad.

She instinctively reached out to him as he walked
away from her without a backward glance. When
he stiffened and paused briefly, she held her breath.
But he resumed his departure, moving farther
and farther away from her until he disappeared
into the hospital.

Her hand fell to her lap. She felt an enormous
weight pressing against her chest, and she thought
she might die.

Ten

Despite a taxing day of travel, medical tests, an interview with the hospital's psychologist, and a lengthy phone conversation with her parents, Emma still couldn't fall asleep. She slouched against the pillows plumped behind her, the covers pulled up to her waist as she stared into the semidarkness.

The unfamiliar quiet of Freedom Hall, the section of the hospital reserved for newly liberated Americans in transit to the United States, seemed deafening in contrast to the violent sounds she'd grown accustomed to during captivity.

Emma sighed, hating the fact that she was alone, but hating even more that David had withdrawn from her with such ease. She ached for him, despite his evident change of heart.

Emma reminded herself yet again that being free was enough, but she knew she was lying to herself every time she whispered the words. The feelings of grief that had built up inside her all day now felt like a crushing weight.

She sank lower onto the bed in her private room and closed her eyes, her mind racing a hundred miles a second as she struggled to understand what had happened.

How, she wondered, could he tell her he loved her and then treat her with such casual disregard? How? she asked herself over and over again as she pressed her clenched fists to her sides and tried not to wail like a wounded animal.

After what they'd survived together, why had he retreated into himself and then walked away from her without so much as a backward glance?

"Why? Someone please tell me why?" she whispered. "I don't understand what happened."

Emma opened her fists and massaged her throbbing temples. When the pain failed to recede, she decided to ask one of the nurses stationed down the hall for an aspirin. Straightening, she threw back the covers and slid to the edge of the bed, but she froze when the door to her room swung open.

David paused in the doorway. Her heart pounding like a jackhammer, Emma gripped the edge of the sheet as he stepped into the room, shut the door, locked it, and then moved toward her. He paused at the side of her bed and peered down at her. Tucking his hands into the pockets of his robe, he asked, "How're you feeling?"

Emma's emotional confusion surfaced and gave her voice an angry edge. "Come to check up on me, Major Winslow? It's not necessary, you know. I won't be a burden to you any longer."

"You couldn't be a burden even if you tried, babe."

She heard his fatigue, but she steeled herself against responding to it. "What do you want?"

"You."

"Why?"

"I need you."

Emma flinched. "I needed you today," she reminded him.

"I know."

Her anger quickly faded at the devastating bleakness in his voice. "What's wrong, David?"

"Everything that's happened in the last two and a half months . . ." he began, then paused and gave her a searching look. "Everything that will happen . . ."

David shook his head, seemingly unwilling or unable to continue. Emma couldn't decide which.

"It's a shock to be free, isn't it?" she asked.

He nodded.

She wanted to understand his present state of mind, so she speculated aloud. "It must have hit you all at once."

"Something like that."

"So you're wrestling with what's happened and you're trying to come to terms with it," she reasoned softly. "Is that why you withdrew into yourself today? Is that why you wouldn't talk to me?"

"That's part of it," he conceded quietly.

Emma felt hope spark inside her. "We'll be all right, David, but only if we're patient with ourselves and with each other. We can share what we've experienced. It might help us both."

"I still need you."

She reached out and took his hand so that she could draw him closer, words failing her as tumultuous emotions choked her. She swallowed against the sudden tightness in her throat.

"I'll always need you, babe. That need won't ever go away," he confessed, that familiar roughness back in his voice.

Uncertain, Emma stared up at him. He lifted a hand and brought it to her cheek. She covered his fingers with hers, turned, and brushed her lips across his palm.

"Forgive me?" he asked.

She held her breath for a moment, then nodded. When she felt his hand tremble, the remaining threads of her hurt and resistance snapped. She wanted him as badly as he needed her. Now. That was all that mattered, she told herself.

Whatever the price, she decided she would pay it.

A dim shaft of light from a nearby street lamp allowed them to watch each other. With her gaze fixed on David's rugged features, Emma tugged at the ties of her nightgown and peeled it from her body. David hurriedly stripped off his robe and pajama bottoms. Extending her arms, she welcomed him into her heart and her bed.

His hands shook as he drew her against the heat and power of his already aroused body. Emma gasped, feeling scorched by the skin-to-skin contact.

"Love me, David."

"I do, babe. Oh, God, I do."

Sinking back against the pillows, she wrapped her arms around him in the same split second that she found his mouth. Eager to absorb him into her flesh and ravenous for his taste, she pressed frantic kisses to his chin and mouth before delving past his parted lips and teeth to taste him.

She moaned, a throaty moan that sent a shudder through David that she felt and absorbed. After repeatedly tangling her tongue with his, she sucked the tip between her teeth and worried it with tender bites.

Emma brought her knees up on either side of his hips and nudged her pelvis against the hard shaft trapped between their lower bodies. She became increasingly desperate to have him inside her, her body growing moist and pleading and painfully needy.

He responded without hesitation, thrusting into her, withdrawing almost completely, and then thrusting even more deeply. All the while he caressed her breasts and teased her nipples to hard points of fire-filled desire.

Tightening spirals of burning sensation enveloped her, and she expressed her pleasure with gasping little cries and clutching hands.

David advanced and retreated, advanced and retreated. Again and again and again, invading and claiming her as his own.

Wildly aroused, Emma writhed beneath him, the emotional highs and lows she'd experienced that day and well into the night completely forgotten.

Relentless in his quest to pleasure her, David increased his pace, driving her past coherent thought, beyond sanity, and then into the peaking ecstasy of a shattering climax unlike anything she'd ever known.

She clung to him, breathless, disbelieving and quaking with lingering sensation. David soothed her with stroking fingertips and gentle kisses. Stunned by what she'd just experienced, and also lulled by his tenderness, Emma lay spent beneath him.

He unexpectedly shifted partway down her devastated body. Emma reared up off the pillow, startled when he filled his hands with her still-tingling breasts. She groaned as he closed his mouth around one of her nipples and rolled the other one back and forth between his fingers.

Amazed by David's obvious desire to bring her satisfaction once again, she propped herself up on her elbows. Watching him aroused her, as did her knowledge that he hadn't allowed himself to reach completion yet. She loved him even more, she realized, because of his sensual generosity.

David easily stoked back to a roaring blaze the remaining sparks of her first climax. She trembled beneath his skillful hands and mouth, finally falling back against the pillows behind her as passion consumed her.

Moaning, Emma savored each nip, each sucking pull, and each swipe of his tongue. He provoked a flood of searing sensation that was like liquid heat streaming into her veins. She throbbed and ached between her thighs. Her legs shifted restlessly.

"Please," she whispered, too shaken by her craving to feel him inside her to manage anything more.

He lifted his lips from her beaded nipples and swollen breasts, his expression tender and filled with the promise of fulfillment. Sitting up, he stroked her lower lip with his fingertips, then trailed his fingers from her lips to her chin to the valley between her breasts across her quivering belly and down into the depths of her feminine flesh.

Drawing Emma toward him, he lifted her legs and placed them over his thighs. They faced each other, with his hands cradling her hips. Emma smiled, a wholly feminine smile that promised David every pleasure imaginable. She claimed him with her hands, his searing heat and pulsing hardness instantly branding her skin.

David brought her closer still. Their bodies touched and exchanged a devastatingly intimate kiss.

Emma shivered. She felt swollen and wet and incomplete. She shifted her fingers, skimming up and down the length of him before she let out a raw sound of need that matched the one that escaped David.

Lifting her gaze, she pleaded with him with her eyes.

"Now, babe?"

She sighed. "Now, David."

He lifted her and slid into her with a forceful thrust that left her trembling in his embrace and clinging to his shoulders. His mouth swooped down, demanding and erotic as he ate at her lips.

Emma responded to his consuming passion without inhibition. She wrapped her legs around his hips, and her world pitched and tilted like a storm-tossed sea.

She felt his fingers dig into her hips, and she heard his muffled groan. Sensing he was near the edge and feeling the pressure building higher and higher within her own body, she whispered her love and relinquished herself to the sudden burst of sensation that sent her flying into the heavens.

At her release, he thrust high and hard and deep. When a hoarse cry escaped him, Emma drank it in greedily.

David stiffened suddenly, his maleness pulsing, his essence flooding her, his body shattering.

Emma slumped against his broad chest, resting her forehead against his shoulder. Too spent and too breathless to speak, she pressed her lips to his perspiration-dampened skin.

David eventually found the strength to lower their still-merged bodies to the sheets. Soon after, their breathing became the only discernible sound in the room.

Emma opened her eyes to find David dressed in his pajamas and robe. He stood before the window in her hospital room, his expression remote. The dawn was slowly lighting the sky, and she heard a hint of the morning activity taking place beyond the door.

"Good morning," she said. "Have you been awake long?" When he said nothing, she frowned. "David?"

"Morning, babe."

She sat up, combing her hair back from her face with her fingers as she studied him. Despite her desire to believe that all was well between them again, Emma felt unsettled by his aloofness and physical distance. She reached for her discarded nightgown and slipped into it.

"What kind of day is it?" she asked.

David turned finally and looked at her. He made no move to approach her, though. Nor did he answer her. Instead he searched her face with a probing gaze that she found disturbing.

"Talk to me, David. Don't shut me out this way."

She watched him close his hands into tight fists. She grew apprehensive when she heard the harsh sound of his breathing. Worried that he was still having trouble adjusting to his newfound freedom, Emma pushed back the covers and swung her legs over the side of the bed.

"Stay where you are," he ordered. "There's something I need to say, and I can't put it off any longer."

A chill passed over her, but she remained perched on the edge of the bed. Watching him, she drew on her robe, then straightened, her pride forbidding her to huddle beneath her renewed fear that she might lose him. "I'm listening, David."

"Once I walk out of this room today, I won't be back. I'm leaving for Washington this morning."

She smiled with relief. "I understand. You've probably got all kinds of debriefing sessions ahead of you. We can get together once—"

"Emma," he interrupted sharply. "You think you love me, but you can't be sure of your feelings. Especially not after what's happened to you."

Startled, she insisted, "I do love you. How can you assume that I don't know what I feel?"

He shook his head. Sadness and strain were etched on his gaunt face, and his eyes were haunted.

"You *think* you love me," he said. "But once your life's back to normal, I probably won't have a place in it except as part of an unwelcome memory. What happened between us would have happened to any couple in our situation. We needed each other. I was your lifeline, just as you were mine. We wound up caring about each other. It was a natural result of our circumstances, but your feelings are bound to change. You can't make a commitment to me based on the sixteen days you spent in hell."

"I trusted you, David." Emma couldn't help it that the words sounded accusatory.

"And I haven't betrayed your trust. I wouldn't do that kind of thing, and you know it."

Do I? she asked herself, so shocked and bewildered by his attitude that she simply stared at him for several moments.

David stayed perfectly still, so still that Emma had the sudden impulse to grab him by the shoulders and shake some life and sense back into him. Instead she asked, "What are you feeling right now?"

"I don't want to play twenty questions."

"What are you feeling, David?"

"Too damn many emotions to even try to name them all, let alone understand them right now."

She paled. "You don't love me, do you? You just said you did because you thought I needed to hear the words."

"I loved you in prison, Emma." He paused, then started to say something more, but in the end he didn't.

"But you don't now."

"Please don't do this to yourself, babe."

"Don't do what?" she asked, anger flaring inside her. "Don't try to understand why you loved me two days ago, but you don't love me today?"

"You don't understand your own emotions right now."

"Quit saying that!" she shouted. "Quit behaving as though I'm incapable of coherent thought just because I spent some time in jail. I lost weight, not my mind!"

"You're making this more difficult than it has to be."

"No, I'm not. I'm just trying to understand, and I think I do now."

"Is it so hard to comprehend the fact that I'm not sure if what we feel is right or not?" he asked.

"Is it so difficult for you to believe that I don't want either one of us to make a mistake in judgment that could have disastrous results?"

"How can you question my feelings?" she demanded. "How can you doubt me this way? You know me, David, probably better than anyone."

"I have to question your emotions because there's too much at stake here. Are your feelings real enough to endure living the life of a gypsy? How do you think you'll react if you're uprooted every two or three years? Are your feelings real enough to get you through weeks, maybe even months, of being by yourself when I'm deployed?

"Are your feelings real enough for you to be separated for long periods of time from your family and friends? Can you find a way to maintain your commitment to Child Feed and still be a part of my life? What would you do if you had to face a pregnancy alone? Can you handle sharing your life with a man who could go to war tomorrow?" He paused. When she said nothing, he reminded her, "My life is very real, Emma. I've already had one wife who couldn't handle the reality of it all. Surely you can see that we both need time to be certain that our feelings for each other are strong enough to withstand the pressures of my career. Surely you can see that."

She stiffened, humiliated that he could reduce the emotions they'd shared to simple happenstance and hurt that he would minimize her ability to make a commitment to him in spite of the demands of his career.

"What I see is that you obviously feel trapped," she said. "There's no need. I love you, David. I probably always will, but I don't intend to pressure you, nor will I crawl or beg in order to demonstrate the sincerity of my emotions. Another man in my life thought I should behave that way. He was very disappointed when I didn't. You will be, too, if that's what you expect of me right now."

"That's just my point. I don't expect anything of you. I haven't the right."

"I gave you the right," she whispered, "the first time we made love, and every other time since then. Do you think I shared myself with you because I was simply curious about your skill as a lover? Didn't it even occur to you that I wouldn't have become intimate with you if I hadn't loved you?"

As if he were talking to himself, David murmured, "I can't be swayed by anything you say or by the pain I'm causing you." Then he stubbornly shook his head and crossed the room. With his hand resting on the doorknob, he looked back at her. "You and I cannot build a life together on the basis of a negative experience. It won't work. We're both bright enough to know how uncertain emotions can be, even under the best of circumstances."

"I don't believe any of this."

David gripped the doorknob until his knuckles whitened. "One of us has to think clearly. Your feelings for me are the result of a life-and-death crisis situation. At the very least you deserve time to come to terms with being imprisoned and the emotional link you believe you feel with me. There's nothing even remotely normal about what we just went through, so how can you possibly think your feelings are normal? I owe you time, Emma. Time to understand what you really feel. I intend to give you that time, whether or not you want it. I also owe myself time."

"Is this your idea of being honorable, Major Winslow?"

He flinched, his hazel eyes filled with icy shards of green and brown. "Yes, it is. I'm sorry you don't understand how important this is for us both."

"It doesn't matter that I love you?"

"Of course love matters," he replied.

But not my love for you, she realized. Emma knew David well enough to realize that he wouldn't bend. He obviously believed what he was saying, so she stopped trying to persuade him of the depth of her feelings for him. She understood rejection, she reminded herself. She'd experienced it once before, but she couldn't remember feeling so totally disabled.

Slipping from the bed, Emma smoothed her robe into place and then yanked the tie belt at her waist. She lifted her chin and looked at David. Whatever empathy she felt for him only minutes ago disappeared. She consciously buried it beneath the wreckage of their relationship before she said in as steady a voice as she could manage, "This conversation is over. Have a nice life."

Emma jerked when she heard a crisp, oddly patterned knock at the door. *Let it be Sam,* she prayed.

David frowned, his eyes sweeping hungrily over her one final time before he pulled open the door. A tall, dark-haired, meticulously groomed man in his mid-thirties stood in the hallway. He wore a three-piece charcoal-gray suit that shouted Armani and held a bouquet of fresh flowers. Grinning widely, he stepped into the room.

"Sam . . ." Emma took a step forward, then another.

"Be well, babe," David said quietly.

Emma paled and stumbled to a stop. Her eyes darted to his face. "Don't ever call me that again."

David's jaw hardened. After nodding at Emma's visitor, who watched the byplay between Emma and David with frank interest, he exited the room, spine stiff, hands clenched at his sides, and emotion blurring his vision.

"Hey, baby sister, who's your tough-looking friend?"

Emma blinked back the tears stinging her eyes. "He's not a friend. He was, however, in the cell next to mine. We escaped together."

"Marine Corps Major David Winslow, I take it. The media people are chafing at the bit to get at him. He's big news. Bona fide hero material, from what I hear. They'll want a piece of you, too, but you don't look up to a press conference." Sam strolled across the room and placed the bouquet on the nightstand. "Winslow may not be your friend, but he obviously cares about you."

Emma shivered and then squared her shoulders. "You're wrong, Sam. You couldn't be more wrong. I may love him, but he doesn't love me enough to trust my feelings for him. He thinks I'm suffering from some bizarre form of Stockholm syndrome."

Sam flashed a sympathetic glance in her direction and didn't try to change her mind. Pulling her into his arms, he hugged her. "You gonna be okay?"

Emma trembled and held on to him. Resting her forehead against his chest, she sighed brokenly. "Physically, I'm fine."

"How about a good meal and then some first-class shopping? Mom said you'd need lots of good food and a new wardrobe once the doctors declared you fit to travel."

She nodded as she moved out of his embrace, slipped across the room to stand before the window, and idly fingered the slats of the blind.

"Emma?"

A tear slid down her cheek, then another, but she responded to the brotherly worry in his voice when she turned to face him. "Take me home, Sam. I need to feel safe again."

And loved, she thought, her heart so hollow, it hurt with every beat. *I need to feel loved. If not by David, then by my family.*

Eleven

"Emmaline, if you don't snap out of this depression fairly soon, I'm going to insist that you see Dr. Frasier. Perhaps he can do for you what the rest of us have failed to do."

Emma gripped the telephone until her knuckles turned white. She knew her mother's concern was legitimate. She'd been wandering around like a lost puppy since returning to southern California the previous month.

Her parents were worried sick about her, her sister kept threatening to deck the first Marine Corps officer who crossed her path, and her brother called at least every other day from Paris to check up on her. She shuddered just thinking about his phone bills.

"For the record, no one's failed me, and I'm not depressed. Just kind of sad."

"Anger's the next stage, and you're darn close," Mrs. Hamilton cautioned. "So prepare yourself for it, darling."

Emma nodded. "You know me too well, Mom, but quit worrying. I'll bounce back. I always do."

"As I see it, you've got two choices. Either find the man and talk some sense into him, or get on with your life without him. There's no middle ground in this situation."

"David doesn't want me. He's made that very clear."

"Then he's a fool, and you're better off without him."

"He's not a fool, just very strong-willed."

"Stubborn," her mother decided. "That particular personality trait can be hell on a woman's emotions."

Emma laughed, recalling the noisy confrontations of her childhood between her very emotional mother and her very determined father. Their personalities frequently clashed, but they'd never stopped loving each other. Not ever.

"That observation sounds like personal experience talking," she teased.

"Now don't get me started on your mule-headed father. There are times when talking to that man is like trying to communicate with a rock, but I love him. I guess thirty-seven years of accommodating his little quirks has become something of a habit." She changed the subject. "Let's have lunch tomorrow. I can get away from the gallery around one."

Emma smiled, aware of her mother's food preference. "Chinese?"

"What else? Double Happiness Inn at one, then. I'll put it in my book."

"Give Dad a hug for me."

"You could do that yourself if you'd drop by this evening."

"Maybe later in the week," Emma hedged. "Dad will try to talk me into going back to work. I'm not ready yet."

"You wouldn't have to take any trips back to the Middle East."

"That's not the problem, and you already know my feelings on that subject. Our work there is important, and I refuse to be intimidated by bullies and thugs. It's just that I want a little more time to myself. I really need it."

Her mother finally admitted defeat. "All right, darling. Take care. And remember, no more moping around. It's not healthy. Try out that new cookbook I gave you, or go shopping for some clothes. You need a cocktail dress for the Child Feed fund-raiser next month. If those ideas don't appeal to you, call your sister and make a date to see a movie."

She knew she wasn't ready to take any of her mother's advice. "Thanks, Mom. I love you."

Replacing the receiver, Emma felt torn between gratitude to her supportive family and the aching sense of loss she still felt. She loved David, perhaps even more now than when they'd parted.

Two weeks of pampering by her mother and sleeping in her old bedroom at home, as well as another two weeks of privacy in her beachfront cottage, hadn't changed her feelings or her needs. Wandering into the kitchen, Emma paused in front of the glass sliding door.

Her gaze drifted across a wide stretch of deserted beach to linger on the white-capped ocean. It was unseasonably cold for March; an advancing storm had already darkened the sky and made the ocean swells appear angry and threatening.

Emma abruptly turned away from the view. Suddenly very dissatisfied with herself, she knew she couldn't continue mourning the loss of someone who was now a part of her past.

"I'm pining away like some helpless female in a Victorian novel, which is absolutely stupid and amazingly self-destructive," she said to her empty kitchen. "I want *me* back, and I want my life back."

Seizing a plastic bucket, Emma filled it with warm water and detergent, then located the sponge mop. She needed activity, she told herself as she dunked the mop into the bucket and then squeezed it.

"So I'll clean!" she announced with the relief of finally finding an outlet for all the pent-up emotions tumbling around inside. "I may be losing my mind at the moment, but I'll clean until this place shines and then I'll go back to work. You're finished messing with my emotions, David Winslow. Do you hear me, Major? You're finished!"

After mopping the kitchen floor, she moved into the hallway, the tails of her long silk shirt slapping against her legs like punctuation marks to her anger.

Intent on her task, she jumped at the sound of someone pounding on her front door. Propping the mop against the wall, Emma marched to the door, jerked it open—and was stunned to discover David on her doorstep.

He looked different, she decided as she caught her breath and braced herself with a hand against the doorframe. Dressed in casual slacks, an open-necked shirt, and a leather bomber jacket that looked like the real thing, David had a rested, healthy, and properly fed look about him.

As they stood there, a sudden gust of rain spattered minute drops across his shoulders and in his hair, which was now close cropped and seemed an even darker shade of mahogany. His hazel eyes had lost their shadows of fatigue, and, if it was possible, his clean-shaven jaw appeared even more sturdy than she recalled.

Just looking at him made her go all fluttery inside. She instantly resented her response to him, but she doubted she could do much about it. Her gaze narrowed as she noted the stack of wrapped packages in his arms and the half-smile on his rugged face.

"Making a delivery?" she asked flippantly, her anger still sparking like live wires inside her despite her impulse to fling herself into his arms and hold on until the whole world disappeared.

"Only if you're accepting them."

"I don't know that I should."

He angled his head to one side, his gaze speculative but his expression clearly stating that it was up to her whether he would go or stay.

Apparently willing to wait for her decision, he

stood there and watched her. He behaved as though the sky was simply weeping lightly and not in the process of unleashing a storm that would likely last through the night. He smiled suddenly, and Emma felt a flush sweep through her entire body.

"Maybe I should get my umbrella," he commented, his eyes darkly serious despite the grin lifting the corners of his lips.

She slowly shook her head and stepped aside, watching that easy-on-the-eyes, loose-limbed walk of his as he strolled into her living room, deposited the gaily wrapped packages onto the couch, and then shed his leather jacket.

"I wasn't expecting company." She closed the door and fidgeted with the collar of her shirt while he glanced around approvingly at the contemporary decor of the cottage.

"I was afraid to call. I figured you'd refuse to see me."

Her eyes widened. David Winslow afraid?

"Feel like giving me the nickel tour?"

"Maybe later," she answered quietly.

He wandered to the wall of windows on the far side of the room. Like the kitchen, the living room overlooked the ocean. "This was worth the airfare from Washington." He exhaled, his broad shoulders shifting as Emma studied the strong, lean lines of his body. He glanced back at her. "Looks like it's getting bad out there. My flight was almost diverted to Los Angeles because of the weather."

She slowly inched into the room. "You flew out here today?"

He nodded and shoved his hands into his trouser pockets. "Just landed about an hour ago."

"How did you find me?"

David shrugged. "It wasn't hard. You gave me enough to go on."

"Why are you here, David?"

"I missed you. Thought I'd stop in and say hello."

"This isn't exactly your backyard."

"It will be in another month or so."

Emma frowned, not sure of his meaning. "I don't understand."

"I'll be stationed about sixty miles north of here."

"The Marine Corps Air Station at El Toro?"

He smiled in reply.

She trembled under the impact of that potent smile. "Then you're here to apartment-hunt."

His smile faded. "I'll be here for two or three years, so I may buy a place."

She watched him move into the center of the room and saw what appeared to be a flash of stark vulnerability in his eyes. When it disappeared, she wondered if she was imagining things. She shifted nervously, but hunger for him rose up inside her, and warmth stroked the most sensitive parts of her body with invisible fingertips.

She felt David's gaze glide downward to her braless breasts. Emma resisted the urge to cover them with her hands when her nipples tightened and tingled. She drew in an uneven breath, then another, but she managed to ask, "Would you like a drink?"

David nodded once and turned back to the windows instead of watching her flee the room. All his nerve endings sizzled with desire, but her reaction to his arrival saddened him. He felt her hesitation and uncertainty and knew he was the cause. He shifted, trying with little success to ease the pressure building in his loins. He wanted her in his life with an intensity that still had the power to shock him.

"David?"

Although he heard Emma whisper his name a few minutes later, David allowed himself a moment to inhale and then exhale slowly. He ached for her now in the same way that he'd ached for her every day and every night for a solid month. Finally mastering his body, he turned, met her curious gaze, and accepted the mug of beer she held out to him.

"Make yourself comfortable." Emma slipped away on bare feet and took a seat at one end of the couch.

David followed her, but sat at the opposite end of the long couch, the stack of packages like a barrier between them. He took a sip of beer before placing the mug on the coffee table. "How've you been?"

"Lonely. Hurt. Angry," she answered with her typical candor.

"Me too."

"You were right, David."

Alert to the challenge in her voice, he asked, "Right about what?"

"My feelings for you did change."

He nodded, but he died a little inside. "I thought they might."

Bringing her bare feet up, Emma wrapped her arms around her legs and placed her chin on her knees. "What are you really doing here?"

He smiled faintly. "You promised me a birthday bash. I thought I'd collect on your promise."

She glanced at the packages. "You don't give presents on your birthday. You receive them."

"Old Montana tradition. I brought my own."

She smiled in spite of herself. "I'll have to trust you."

"You did before," he reminded her. "Perhaps you will again one day." He selected a package and handed it to her. "This one's for you."

Bemused, she straightened and accepted his offering. After unwrapping and opening the box, Emma discovered a sapphire silk teddy in the folds of tissue paper. "It's beautiful," she whispered, startled that he would give her such an intimate garment.

David handed her a second package. "This one's for you too. Go ahead and open it."

She did and found an ankle-length white lace nightie. Her fingers trembled as she ran them across the delicate material. "This is so extravagant."

"One more," he said, handing her the largest package.

"All right." She gasped and lifted a black silk peignoir from the box. "I don't understand."

"There's nothing to understand. This is my birthday celebration. You said we'd celebrate it together, so we are."

"But these gifts are for a woman."

He shook his head. "They're for you, Emma. Only you."

"You aren't making any sense."

He smiled so sadly that she gripped the peignoir to keep from reaching out to him.

"When a man's being honorable, he doesn't always make a lot of sense. Even when he's trying to."

"I'm not sure what this is all leading up to, so why don't you tell me the real reason for your visit."

"There's no point. You told me your feelings had changed."

She nodded. Stubbornness glinted in her eyes. "They have."

He frowned at the odd expression on her face. "How have your feelings changed, Emma?"

His rough voice sent chills across her skin, but she consciously set aside her reaction to the sound and to his nearness. Because she knew she had nothing left to lose, she searched for and found the courage to risk the truth. "My feelings for you are stronger and far deeper than before."

A muscle worked in his jaw. "Say that again, babe."

"I love you more now than I loved you the last time I saw you." She made sure there was a clear warning in her voice that no one could ever persuade her otherwise. "I told you once that I would always love you, David. What I didn't realize was just how encompassing that love would become."

He got up, crossed the room, and reached for his jacket. Emma froze. For a moment she thought he intended to simply walk out of her life again.

Plucking an item from the inside pocket of his leather jacket, David retraced his steps and paused in front of Emma. He extended his hand and drew her up to stand in front of him. "This is my present to myself, but it won't mean much if you don't like it."

She fumbled with the small velvet-covered box when he unexpectedly dropped it in the palm of her hand. As she was about to open it, her nerves got the best of her, and she changed her mind. "I can't."

He held very still. "You don't want it?"

She shook her head as she stared at the velvet container. "It's not that. I'm just nervous. I don't want to drop it, whatever it is."

David smiled. "I'm nervous too." He accepted the box, snapped it open, and turned it so that Emma could see the pear-cut diamond in a gold engagement setting. A matching wedding band studded with smaller pear-cut diamonds rested next to it.

"Oh, my," Emma whispered as she glanced from the rings to David's face and then back at the rings. "They're beautiful."

"I love you, Emma Hamilton. Will you marry me?"

She walked straight into his arms, slipped her arms around his waist, and held on to him. She savored the feel of his muscular chest, flat belly, and powerful thighs as she molded herself to him. "You shouldn't have sent me away. It was an insane thing to do. We needed each other."

"I didn't want to leave you, babe, but I believed it was the right thing to do when I did it. You needed time alone. So did I."

"An entire month?" Emma groaned as she looked up at him. "It's been awful."

"Try to understand," he said. "When my ex-wife left me, I swore I'd never let myself love anyone so much that I'd feel like dying if the relationship ended. But that's exactly how I've felt since Germany. Empty and alone. Dead inside."

"It's been that way for me too."

He ground his teeth together and shook his head, his disgust with himself evident. "I was afraid to need you too much, babe, but I did. Every day. Every night. I thought we cared about each other for the wrong reasons, and I believed that once we were free we'd stop needing each other. I was wrong. If anything, I needed and wanted you even more. You were like a beacon of hope for me in prison. You became my strength. I focused on you, and I managed to forget my anger, my hunger, and my pain. You made me laugh, you made me want to cry some of the time, and you made me ache with needs that only you can satisfy."

"But, David—"

"Let me finish, because I want to put this past

month behind us. I thought I loved you, but I wasn't completely certain. I also didn't want to hurt you, but I was damned whatever I did. Sending you away was painful for us both, but I was convinced it was our only option. The minute I got on that plane for Washington, I knew I'd just made the biggest mistake of my life."

"You could've called me. We could have talked."

"I almost did," he admitted. "Several times."

Bewildered, she asked, "What stopped you?"

"I loved you enough not to pressure you when you were putting your life together."

She remembered the emptiness and isolation of the preceding month. Tears welled in her eyes, but she blinked them back. "I didn't think you loved me at all."

David cupped her face with his hands and lowered his lips to hers. He kissed her gently, almost reverently. When he lifted his head, he asked quietly, "How could I not love you? You're all I think about. You're everything I've ever wanted. You're my future, babe. Everything else that's happened is in the past, and I want it to stay that way."

He wrapped his arms around her, nearly crushing her within his embrace as he seared the side of her neck and her face with hot kisses. "I handled the whole situation very badly, but I needed you to be sure. I meant it when I said it wasn't easy to marry a man in military aviation. There are a lot of sacrifices involved. I've already had one relationship go up in smoke because of my work, and I can't bear the thought of another failed marriage."

She tenderly stroked the side of his face with her fingertips. "David, I love you enough to understand your career and live with it. I'm also enough of an individual to maintain my own interests. And that includes Child Feed, because I don't intend to abandon my work."

He looked down at her. "I honestly believed that you were too fragile to know your own mind or to understand your true feelings about us by the time we arrived in Germany. I guess I didn't understand the kind of emotional commitment you were making to me when we made love. I even convinced myself that your feelings for me probably wouldn't last once your life got back to normal. Now I know I was wrong. I wound up hurting you when all I was trying to do was what was best for you. Can you ever forgive me for what I've put us through?"

She smiled. Forgiveness came easily because she now understood that they'd both paid a painfully high price for their time apart. He'd had the best intentions, she realized, no matter how misguided.

"It doesn't matter how or where or why we fell in love, David. It just matters that we love each other enough to make a lifetime commitment. I have enormous faith in us. I have since those first minutes in my cell when you cared enough to ask me if I was all right."

"I realize that now. Believe me, I've had more lonely hours than I care to think about." He took the engagement ring from the box and slipped it onto her finger. "I need an answer, babe."

"Do you promise always to talk to me before you do what you think's best for me?" she asked, the teasing in her voice softening the difficult question.

He nodded, his expression serious.

"Do you promise to assume that I will love you regardless of what you do for a living?"

He smiled. "I promise."

"Do you promise to trust me when I tell you that I love you?"

"Always, babe."

"And do you promise to love me forever and to make beautiful babies with me?"

He kissed her soundly and then whispered against her lips, "With pleasure. Now say you'll marry me."

She leaned back, but he kept their lower bodies fitted together. She pressed even closer to the obvious strength of his desire for her. "Yes, David, I'll marry you."

Emma welcomed his embrace and his lips. Savoring the consuming fire of David's loving passion, she knew with utter certainty that both his love and his passion for her would last a lifetime.

THE EDITOR'S CORNER

If there were a theme for next month's LOVESWEPTs, it might be "Pennies from Heaven," because in all six books something unexpected and wonderful seems to drop from above right into the lives of our heroes and heroines.

First, in **MELTDOWN,** LOVESWEPT #558, by new author Ruth Owen, a project that could mean a promotion at work falls into Chris Sheffield's lap. He'll work with Melanie Rollins on fine-tuning her superintelligent computer, Einstein, and together they'll reap the rewards. It's supposed to be strictly business between the handsome rogue and the brainy inventor, but then white-hot desire strikes like lightning. Don't miss this heartwarming story—and the humorous jive-talking, TV-shopping computer—from one of our New Faces of '92.

Troubles and thrills crash in on the heroine's vacation in Linda Cajio's **THE RELUCTANT PRINCE,** LOVESWEPT #559. A coup breaks out in the tiny country Emily Cooper is visiting, then she's kidnapped by a prince! Alex Kiros, who looks like any woman's dream of Prince Charming, has to get out of the country, and the only way is with Emily posing as his wife—a masquerade that has passionate results. Treat yourself to this wildly exciting, very touching romance from Linda.

Lynne Marie Bryant returns to LOVESWEPT with **SINGULAR ATTRACTION,** #560. And it's definitely singular how dashing fly-boy Devlin King swoops down from the skies, barely missing Kristi Bjornson's plane as he lands on an Alaskan lake. Worse, Kristi learns that Dev's family owns King Oil, the company she opposes in her work to save tundra swans. Rest assured, though, that Dev finds a way to mend their differences and claim her heart. This is pure romance set amid the wilderness beauty of the North. Welcome back, Lynne!

In **THE LAST WHITE KNIGHT** by Tami Hoag, LOVE-SWEPT #561, controversy descends on Horizon House, a halfway home for troubled girls. And like a golden-haired Sir Galahad, Senator Erik Gunther charges to the rescue, defending counselor Lynn Shaw's cause with compassion. Erik is the soul mate she's been looking for, but wouldn't a woman with her past tarnish his shining armor? Sexy and sensitive, **THE LAST WHITE KNIGHT** is one more superb love story from Tami.

The title of Glenna McReynolds's new LOVESWEPT, **A PIECE OF HEAVEN,** #562, gives you a clue as to how it fits into our theme. Tired of the rodeo circuit, Travis Cayou returns to the family ranch and thinks a piece of heaven must have fallen to earth when he sees the gorgeous new manager. Callie Michaels is exactly the kind of woman the six-feet-plus cowboy wants, but she's as skittish as a filly. Still, Travis knows just how to woo his shy love. . . . Glenna never fails to delight, and this vibrantly told story shows why.

Last, but never the least, is Doris Parmett with **FIERY ANGEL,** LOVESWEPT #563. When parachutist Roxy Harris tumbles out of the sky and into Dennis Jorden's arms, he knows that Fate has sent the lady just for him. But Roxy insists she has no time to tangle with temptation. Getting her to trade a lifetime of caution for reckless abandon in Dennis's arms means being persistent . . . and charming her socks off. **FIERY ANGEL** showcases Doris's delicious sense of humor and magic touch with the heart.

On sale this month from FANFARE are three fabulous novels and one exciting collection of short stories. Once again, *New York Times* bestselling author Amanda Quick returns to Regency England with **RAVISHED.** Sweeping from a cozy seaside village to the glittering ballrooms of fashionable London, this enthralling tale of a thoroughly mismatched couple poised to discover the rapture of love is Amanda Quick at her finest.

Three beloved romance authors combine their talents in **SOUTHERN NIGHTS,** an anthology of three original novellas that present the many faces of unexpected love. Here are *Summer Lightning* by Sandra Chastain, *Summer Heat* by Helen Mittermeyer, and *Summer Stranger* by Patricia Potter—stories that will make you shiver with the timeless passion of **SOUTHERN NIGHTS.**

In **THE PRINCESS** by Celia Brayfield, there is talk of what will be the wedding of the twentieth century. The groom is His Royal Highness, Prince Richard, wayward son of the House of Windsor. But who will be his bride? From Buckingham Palace to chilly Balmoral, **THE PRINCESS** is a fascinating look into the inner workings of British nobility.

The bestselling author of three highly praised novels, Ann Hood has fashioned an absorbing contemporary tale with **SOMETHING BLUE.** Rich in humor and wisdom, it tells the unforgettable story of three women navigating through the perils of romance, work, and friendship.

Also from Helen Mittermeyer is **THE PRINCESS OF THE VEIL,** on sale this month in the Doubleday hardcover edition. With this breathtakingly romantic tale of a Viking princess and a notorious Scottish chief, Helen makes an outstanding debut in historical romance.

Happy reading!

With warmest wishes,

Nita Taublib
Associate Publisher
LOVESWEPT and FANFARE

Don't miss these fabulous
Bantam Fanfare titles
on sale in JUNE

SOUTHERN NIGHTS
by Sandra Chastain, Helen Mittermeyer,
and Patricia Potter

RAVISHED
by Amanda Quick

THE PRINCESS
by Celia Brayfield

SOMETHING BLUE
by Ann Hood

And in hardcover from Doubleday,
PRINCESS OF THE VEIL
by Helen Mittermeyer

SOUTHERN NIGHTS

by your favorite LOVESWEPT authors:
Sandra Chastain, Helen Mittermeyer,
and Patricia Potter

*Sultry, caressing, magnolia-scented breezes . . .
sudden, fierce thunderstorms . . . nights of beauty
and enchantment. In three original novellas, favorite
LOVESWEPT authors present the many faces of summer and unexpected love.*

*SUMMER LIGHTNING by Sandra Chastain is the
story of a man and woman in Nashville, and the
midnight dream of healing and love that they share.*

She moved quietly across the patio, through the open
glass doors, and into the room. Intent on his music, the
singer never heard her bare feet on the polished wood
floor. He didn't hear the piano seat sigh as she sat down
and waited.

As if she were inside his mind, she felt his frustration,
understood the emotion he was searching for. And when
he reached the point where his notes stopped, she put
her fingers on the piano keys and completed the refrain.

There was a long silence.

The man laid his guitar down on the floor and stood.
"Who are you?"

I don't know yet, she could have whispered. But that answer, like the music, remained within some secret part of her, and instead she said softly, "My name is Summer."

"Summer. Summer who appears in the dark of the night, bringing beauty and music to a man who badly needs both?"

Scars forgotten in the shadows, she moved toward him, drawn not only by his need but by hers and the compelling connection that seemed to join them. There was a sensual power to the man, more potent at close range than from a distance. "Yes. You called out to me. I've been listening."

"I know. I don't know how, but I felt your presence. How could you know the end to my song?"

He'd come close enough for the light from behind her to flicker against his face. He was tall and thin, too thin. His face was hollowed as if he were very tired, and his dark hair was combed back from his face.

There was an eerie understanding between them, a rightness that caught and held her. She had no urge to turn and flee. "I—I don't know," she admitted. "Does it matter?"

"Summer," the man repeated. "No, it doesn't matter. You're part of the music of the night. Come closer." He held out his hand.

She hesitated, drawn to the man by some unexplainable urge, yet unable to step into the light. She didn't flinch when his hand gently encircled her wrist.

"You're trembling," he said. "Don't be afraid of me. Don't ever be afraid of me."

"I'm not," she explained. "I think that I'm afraid of me." He continued to hold her hand, but he remained at arm's length, as if he were allowing her to get used to his presence.

"An earring?" she asked, catching its glitter in the light. A dream, she could have said as she took a step closer to touch his face.

"Barefoot?" he asked, touching her foot with his own. Beautiful, he could have said, for though he couldn't fully see it, he could feel her beauty. In the gray, velvety shadows she stood like a ghostly vision, pale and shimmering in the half-light. Even her skin glowed. Whatever she was wearing caught the light and gave off an aura of silver.

The air was heavy and smothering. Closer now came the loud rumble of sound, followed by a flash of lightning. A quick, brisk wind suddenly swept through the pine trees with the sound of a long whisper, ruffling the magnolia leaves and slamming a door inside the house, plunging the room into darkness.

She took in a quick breath.

He pulled her closer, and when he put his arms around her, she felt comforted. As the rain began to fall in the garden beyond, she leaned her face against his chest. The beat of his heart matched the rhythm of the approaching storm.

She felt as though she were in a dream, as she had when she'd woken in that hospital bed. But that dream was cold, and this dream was alive with warmth. She didn't know who this man was, but she'd stopped asking questions for which there were no answers. Wherever she was, she was supposed to be there. She'd been expected, though neither of them had known. She'd brought him answers to questions he'd voiced through his music. And he was offering her solace.

She smelled the rain. The still, heavy humidity of a Southern storm wrapped them in a sensual heat. She felt his chest hair against her breasts with every breath.

Silk, he thought. She was wearing some little wispy silk thing with thin, nothing straps and a bottom that barely came to her thighs. It was soft and slippery, moving silently between their bodies. Her hair was very long, brushing against the back of his hands as he caressed her bottom.

His left leg twinged, and he shifted his weight to the right one, the movement bringing his knee between her legs. She wasn't wearing anything beneath the silk. The thought stole his breath away.

The thunder rumbled closer. The lightning pierced the darkness, and the rain fell. As if in a dream, he lifted her in his arms.

"What?"

"Shush." He hushed her question with his lips, lips that spoke of loneliness and gentle caring, lips that promised refuge from the storm.

And with his touch her past faded out of her mind. The lonely pain, the pure frustration of being totally controlled, all disappeared with his touch. In the darkness she gave in to her pent-up longings. She slipped her arms around his neck and parted her lips to taste him. For this night it didn't matter who he was. It didn't matter who she was. It mattered only that they were two people who needed each other.

Helen Mittermeyer's SUMMER HEAT takes place in the land of the steamy and mysterious Louisiana bayou, where a woman struggling to rebuild her life amid the decayed splendor of her ancestral home is joined by a most unexpected visitor—her husband.

Now they would meet again. He was through waking up in the night, believing her next to him. And he was damned sure, after the divorce, he would be able to force her from his mind completely.

Hunching over, relying on the rain-streaked car windows as cover, he waited until the last second before pressing the button to lower the window. "Hello, Zane."

Luckily he had quick reflexes and ducked when she swung at him. The force of her swing brought her hand in the open window and he grabbed her wrist.

"Do I pull you in through the window?" he asked. "Or would you like to enter by the door?"

Rain pelted them steadily, soaking his one arm and dampening the rest of him.

Shock sent Zane reeling. She couldn't really believe it was Jake. He'd walked in her mind so much, he could have been a wraith, a figment of her imagination. No such luck. He was there, inches from her, her nemesis, her onetime boss, her erstwhile husband, and father of her two children . . . but he didn't know that. She'd always had the feeling this day would come. Time to contact her lawyer and fight any claim he could make. And she'd battle him too.

But fighting Jake was a tenuous position at best. He knew all the moves. She'd need more armor than she had.

Staying hidden from him had seemed her most viable alternative, though she'd often questioned the rightness of it. Many times she'd longed for him so deeply, it was a physical pain. As the days pushed into weeks, though, as she learned about her pregnancy, her reluctance to contact him deepened and hardened. After a while, too much time had passed. She knew she couldn't return, even if she wished. She'd come to think of herself as safe. Now he was here. She swallowed, her body trembling with all the fears she'd lived with for almost four years.

"I'll come in the door," she said tautly.

"Fine." Jake kept hold of her wrist as he opened the door and stepped out into the rain. He took her other hand, intending to pull her into the car with him, but stopped. Touching her was an unexpected stunner. She still had the power to melt his intentions and his knees. Fiercely reminding himself why he was there, he urged her into the car. She tried to pull free of his hold.

"Wouldn't it be easier for me to go around instead of crawling over the seat?"

"You're getting wetter as we argue."

"So are you," she shot back, feeling childish.

"C'mon, Zane," he said, amusement overriding his irritation. She'd always been able to do that to him too. She could make him laugh as no one else could.

"Don't drag me." She finally managed to free her hands and clambered over the driver's seat and the console, settling into the passenger seat. He slid back into the car and slammed the door shut. Enclosed in the small space with him, Zane couldn't get her breath. He'd always had that effect on her—and probably every other woman he met. But all that was behind her now. She didn't want anything to do with him. Why was he in Louisiana? And why now? She'd begun to wash him from her life. Whole days went by when she didn't think of him. She was happy. Her life was full. What unhappy Fate had brought him here?

Few outsiders appeared in Isabella. Her business was through the mail, and she used a pen name. She'd kept a low profile all these years, so how had he found her?

"What are you doing in Isabella?" she asked.

Jake didn't answer. He barely heard her as he stared at her. He hadn't expected her to still be so beautiful. No, more beautiful. Even without makeup, her clothing and hair dripping wet, she was still lovelier. There was a fullness to her now, a deepening, ripening to her lissome beauty. She should have been a model, not a business major with an art minor; a movie star, not a talented sketcher. He could recall the many times she'd done him in charcoal. She was good. Had she burned those sketches? Acid twisted his guts.

He'd expected his fury, but the surge of passion rocked him. Just glancing at her had his body hardening, the want swelling like a flood. Damn her! It was over. Maybe it had even been over before she left. So why the hell should he still want her?

SUMMER STRANGERS by Patricia Potter is an enchanting story of seductive summer magic and the fiery opulence of Fourth of July fireworks in Georgia that turn a sensible woman reckless, sending her into the arms of a laughing, impulsive man.

She didn't see Patrick until she mounted the stairs to her second-floor apartment and found him sprawled across the top step, his eyes consuming what appeared to be a camping magazine. At the sound of her approach his gaze immediately turned upward to her face, and she saw his eyes spark in a way that warmed her heart.

Corey was surprised at how loudly her heart thumped. This had been a terribly discouraging day, and now unaccountably the afternoon had suddenly brightened.

Patrick with no last name. Patrick with eyes that laughed. Patrick the musician. Patrick who apparently had few interests outside his own pleasures. The kind of man she'd never thought would attract her, much less hold any fascination for her.

But now she was captivated by him, by his presence, by the crazy things he made her feel inside, by the inexplicable happiness he suddenly brought just by being here.

Be careful, Corey.

But though the warning ran loud and clear through her mind, she wasn't listening. A churning had started deep within her body, a physical yearning so strong, it nearly overwhelmed her.

"Hi," she said, trying to keep the trembling from her voice. A longer greeting was beyond her at this moment.

He grinned at her, that open devil-may-care smile that denied any troubles in the world. He straightened up, and his eyes perused her, from the high heels all the way up to the blouse buttoned nearly to her neck and then to the briefcase in her hand.

He shook his head slowly, and Corey wondered whether it was censure about her working on a Saturday or disappointment with her, now that he was seeing her without benefit of the night that softened reality and cast its spell of enchantment.

Except she still felt *it*. Dear God, she still felt every single bit of it. He had the same effect on her today as last night. God help her, this was no dream.

He was all reality this Saturday afternoon. She had seen part of his legs last night, but now she had full view, and full impact. He was wearing white tennis shorts, revealing legs that were a dark, rich bronze and muscular. There was incredible strength there. She remembered his telling her about his not playing football, yet she had no doubt now that he was an athlete, natural born and more trained than he cared to admit.

Suddenly embarrassed by what must be a wide-eyed stare at his lower anatomy, she raised her eyes, not that the view lost any of its fascination. He was wearing a light blue knit shirt that contrasted with the bronze color of his arms and the black crinkly hairs revealed by the shirt's open neck. His dark hair was mussed, as if he'd combed it with his fingers, and a crooked smile played havoc with what little sense she had remaining.

"I didn't have your phone number," he explained, his head tipped slightly to one side as if inquiring whether he was welcome.

"I thought . . ." Her words trailed off. She thought *it* had started and ended last night and this morning. But the fantasy was sitting in front of her, and it was no longer a fantasy but a tall, perfectly formed, irresistible reality, with a crooked, uncertain grin that made her heart bounce like a ball.

"You thought . . . ?" he prompted her.

"That you might have been a mirage." She was aware that she was smiling, even more aware that her answer was unusually spontaneous, but then he had that effect on her.

He reached out a hand and took her briefcase, then held her fingers in a warm, possessive clasp. "No mirage," he said. "Believe me, I didn't think such a thing about you."

His look was heated and intense, and didn't seem to go along with everything else about him, with that easygoing personality.

"Are you going to invite me in?"

All the unreality of last night, the lovely gossamer web of magic, wrapped itself around her again, around the two of them. "It depends," she said gently but with searching eyes.

"On what?"

"Whether you are really real or not."

"Oh, I'm very real," he said, accepting the challenge as he leaned over and pressed his lips against hers.

He was so real that he made her body tremble. Summer storm. Summer lightning. Summer thunder. Corey felt all of them and more.

None of the special bewitchery had left with the night. It was even more alive, perhaps because it had survived the harsh test of full daylight. Even as his kiss made her dizzy, she could feel the beat of his heart, the pulsing of a vein in his throat. So real. Yet unreal.

The joy she felt at being with him was unexpected and painful, exquisitely painful, his touch even more so as his kiss deepened until she thought he was going to consume her.

And for the first time in her life, she wanted to be consumed.

PRINCESS OF THE VEIL

by Helen Mittermeyer

*A novel of soaring romance and
thrilling adventure
set in long-ago Scotland*

THE VIKING PRINCESS HID HER PAIN AND BEAUTY BEHIND A VEIL

The faint scar on her face is a symbol of shame—a certainty that she is forever unworthy of love and marriage—and an exotic mark of beauty. Abused and frightened by her Scottish uncle, Iona hates and distrusts all men—especially the Scots. With the courage of a warrior and the vision of a leader, she sails a fleet of ships to her place of birth on the Orkney Islands to create a sanctuary for women.

THE SCOTTISH CHIEFTAIN FACED HIS GREATEST CHALLENGE

The last of the Sinclairs, Magnus desperately needs an heir to secure his right to the land of his ancestors. When his ships defeat Iona's forces in a battle at sea, her pride and beauty as she is brought before him shake him to his soul. She and no other must be his bride . . .

HIS PASSION HELD HER PRISONER . . .
HER BEAUTY HELD HIM SPELLBOUND . . .

To save her crew, Iona is forced to marry the compellingly attractive chieftain. But though she is helpless to resist his passionate possession, she swears he will never break her rebellious Viking spirit.

RAVISHED

by *New York Times* bestselling author
Amanda Quick

*Get ready to be RAVISHED as Amanda Quick makes
those hazy days of summer even hotter!*

"If you had any sense you would run from me as fast as
you possibly could," Gideon Westbrook tells Harriet
Pomeroy. Dubbed the "Beast of Blackthorne Hall"
for his scarred face and lecherous past, Gideon has
been summoned by Harriet to help her rout the un-
scrupulous thieves who are using her beloved caves
to hide their loot. Though others quake before the
strong, fierce, and notoriously menacing Gideon, Harriet cannot find it in her heart to fear him. For she
senses in him a savage pain she longs to soothe . . .
and a searing passion she yearns to answer. Now,
caught up in the beast's clutches, Harriet must find a
way to win his heart—and evade the deadly trap of a
scheming villain who would see them parted for all
time.

Sweeping from a cozy seaside village to glittering
London, this enthralling tale of a thoroughly mismatched couple poised to discover the rapture of love
is Amanda Quick at her finest.

THE PRINCESS

by Celia Brayfield

A DYNAMIC BRITISH PRINCE
In a story that tantalizes from first page to last, Celia Brayfield invites you into the private world behind the glittering facade of modern royalty. THE PRINCESS breaks the unspoken code that has sheltered the British Royal Family from scandal-hungry tabloids around the world.

THE WEDDING OF THE CENTURY
From family suppers at Buckingham Palace to exclusive house parties at chilly Balmoral, THE PRINCESS reveals the lives of Britain's nobility through the eyes of three remarkable women . . . friends from vastly different backgrounds who meet in the cloistered grandeur of Cambridge . . . rivals who vie for the heart of the most eligible bachelor in the world. . . .

BUT WHICH OF THREE CAPTIVATING
WOMEN WILL BE HIS PRINCESS?
He is His Royal Highness, Prince Richard, Duke of Sussex, and wayward son of the House of Windsor. A charismatic man of dominating grace and fierce aspirations, he has known many women. But only three understand him. And now, only one holds the key to unlock the mysteries of his heart.

A MAIN SELECTION OF THE DOUBLEDAY BOOK CLUB.

SOMETHING BLUE

by Ann Hood
author of
SOMEWHERE OFF THE COAST OF MAINE

"At heart it's an engaging, warmly old-fashioned story of the perils and endurance of romance, work, and friendship."—*The Washington Post*

On the morning of her wedding, Katherine leaves her sister a note that reads "If I stay here and do this I think I will die," and shows up on the doorstep of her old college friend Lucy. But Katherine finds herself an unwelcome intrusion. Lucy is too busy coping with her fading love for her boyfriend, her newfound success as an illustrator, and her best friend Julia, who's fearful of romantic commitments. As they strive to create more promising lives for themselves, Lucy and Katherine must learn to forge a new relationship based on the women they have become, while Lucy and Julia must test uneasy new ground in their friendship.

A novel rich in humor and wisdom, SOMETHING BLUE is an unforgettable story crafted in Ann Hood's trademark style—a pitch-perfect sense of character and feel for contemporary culture.

FANFARE

On Sale in June

RAVISHED

☐ 29316-8 $4.99/5.99 in Canada

by Amanda Quick

<u>New York Times</u> bestselling author

Sweeping from a cozy seaside village to glittering London, this enthralling tale of a thoroughly mismatched couple poised to discover the rapture of love is Amanda Quick at her finest.

THE PRINCESS

☐ 29836-4 $5.99

by Celia Brayfield

He is His Royal Highness, the Prince Richard, and wayward son of the House of Windsor. He has known many women, but only three understand him, and only one holds the key to unlock the mysteries of his heart.

SOMETHING BLUE

☐ 29814-3 $5.99/6.99 in Canada

by Ann Hood

Author of SOMEWHERE OFF THE COAST OF MAINE

"An engaging, warmly old-fashioned story of the perils and endurance of romance, work, and friendship." -- <u>The Washington Post</u>

SOUTHERN NIGHTS

☐ 29815-1 $4.99/5.99 in Canada

by Sandra Chastain, Helen Mittermeyer, and Patricia Potter

Sultry, caressing, magnolia-scented breezes. . .sudden, fierce thunderstorms. . .nights of beauty and enchantment. In three original novellas, favorite LOVESWEPT authors present the many faces of summer and unexpected love.

🌀   🌀   🌀

Look for these books at your bookstore or use this page to order.

☐ Please send me the books I have checked above. I am enclosing $ _____ (add $2.50 to cover postage and handling). Send check or money order, no cash or C. O. D.'s please.

Mr./ Ms. _____

Address _____

City/ State/ Zip _____

Send order to: Bantam Books, Dept. FN, 2451 S. Wolf Rd., Des Plaines, IL 60018
Allow four to six weeks for delivery.

Prices and availability subject to change without notice.   FN 52 7/92

FANFARE

Rosanne Bittner

_____ 28599-8 EMBERS OF THE HEART . $4.50/5.50 in Canada
_____ 29033-9 IN THE SHADOW OF THE MOUNTAINS
$5.50/6.99 in Canada
_____ 28319-7 MONTANA WOMAN .... $4.50/5.50 in Canada
_____ 29014-2 SONG OF THE WOLF .... $4.99/5.99 in Canada

Deborah Smith

_____ 28759-1 THE BELOVED WOMAN .. $4.50/ 5.50 in Canada
_____ 29092-4 FOLLOW THE SUN .... $4.99/ 5.99 in Canada
_____ 29107-6 MIRACLE .... $4.50/ 5.50 in Canada

Tami Hoag

_____ 29053-3 MAGIC .... $3.99/4.99 in Canada

Dianne Edouard and Sandra Ware

_____ 28929-2 MORTAL SINS .... $4.99/5.99 in Canada

Kay Hooper

_____ 29256-0 THE MATCHMAKER, ... $4.50/5.50 in Canada
_____ 28953-5 STAR-CROSSED LOVERS .. $4.50/5.50 in Canada

Virginia Lynn

_____ 29257-9 CUTTER'S WOMAN, ... $4.50/4.50 in Canada
_____ 28622-6 RIVER'S DREAM, ... $3.95/4.95 in Canada

Patricia Potter

_____ 29071-1 LAWLESS .... $4.99/ 5.99 in Canada
_____ 29069-X RAINBOW .... $4.99/ 5.99 in Canada

Ask for these titles at your bookstore or use this page to order.

Please send me the books I have checked above. I am enclosing $ _____ (please add
$2.50 to cover postage and handling). Send check or money order, no cash or C. O. D.'s
please.

Mr./ Ms. _____

Address _____

City/ State/ Zip _____

Send order to: Bantam Books, Dept. FN, 414 East Golf Road, Des Plaines, IL 60016
Please allow four to six weeks for delivery.

Prices and availablity subject to change without notice.   FN 17 - 4/92

FANFARE

Sandra Brown

- ❏ 28951-9 TEXAS! LUCKY ....$4.50/$5.50 in Canada
- ❏ 28990-X TEXAS! CHASE ....$4.99/$5.99 in Canada
- ❏ 29500-4 TEXAS! SAGE ....$4.99/$5.99 in Canada
- ❏ 29085-1 22 INDIGO PLACE ....$4.50/$5.50 in Canada

Amanda Quick

- ❏ 28594-7 SURRENDER ....$4.50/$5.50 in Canada
- ❏ 28932-2 SCANDAL ....$4.95/$5.95 in Canada
- ❏ 28354-5 SEDUCTION ....$4.99/$5.99 in Canada
- ❏ 29325-7 RENDEZVOUS ....$4.99/$5.99 in Canada

Deborah Smith

- ❏ 28759-1 THE BELOVED WOMAN ....$4.50/$5.50 in Canada
- ❏ 29092-4 FOLLOW THE SUN ....$4.99/$5.99 in Canada
- ❏ 29107-6 MIRACLE ....$4.50/$5.50 in Canada

Iris Johansen

- ❏ 28855-5 THE WIND DANCER ....$4.95/$5.95 in Canada
- ❏ 29032-0 STORM WINDS ....$4.99/$5.99 in Canada
- ❏ 29244-7 REAP THE WIND ....$4.99/$5.99 in Canada

Available at your local bookstore or use this page to order.

Send to: Bantam Books, Dept. FN 58
          2451 S. Wolf Road
          Des Plaines, IL 60018

Please send me the items I have checked above. I am enclosing
$_____ (please add $2.50 to cover postage and handling). Send
check or money order, no cash or C.O.D.'s, please.

Mr./Ms._____

Address_____

City/State_____Zip_____
Please allow four to six weeks for delivery.
Prices and availability subject to change without notice.   FN 58 7/92